THE
LAST
STRYKER

DARK UNIVERSE SERIES #1

ALEX SHEPPARD

My girls—sugar and spice, not always nice.

THE
LAST
STRYKER

SECTOR 22

The *Endeavor* was not supposed to be anywhere near Sector 22. In a warp of fate, instead of its planned run to Komilah to drop off a crate of Pterostrich eggs, the battlecruiser-turned-freighter was spit out in the middle of nowhere.

Ross Pornell, second-in-command of the *Endeavor*, sat frozen in the captain's chair, staring blankly at the scene outside. They were zooming past a planet with a mottled-orange surface and the system's twin stars were just specks in the distance. Ross didn't know where they were, except for the fact that they weren't supposed to be here.

Even though Ross had never been trained in the gritty ways of the Armed Services of the Confederacy, he was not one to be shaken easily. Not too long ago he had fought against pirates in Sector 79 and had hardly broken a sweat. But the current situation was unexpected, and Ross had to admit—albeit unwillingly—that he hadn't a clue about what to do next. The god-awful klaxon's earsplitting ruckus did nothing to help.

A second or two after *Endeavor's* abrupt arrival in Sector 22 that had set the ship-wide alarm blaring, Ross got some bearing back. He pressed the communications module embedded on the side of his brushed-steel chair. "Flux, why the alarm?" he said over the intercom.

The engineer's hasty, "Running systems check, Ross," drifted in from the engineering bay via the communicator. "All my scans are clear," Flux said a moment later.

Another second or two passed before the alarm died and Ross breathed a sigh of relief. He looked around the semicircular COM or Core Operations Module. It was designed in a rather eclectic fashion and differently from most battlecruisers Ross had seen. Instead of the usual spacious set up with the officers' stations ringing the captain's seat on a central raised deck, Endeavor's dual control stations were simple and sparse. The room was tight, and right now, even with just three people in it, it felt claustrophobic.

"What the hell just happened, Fenny?" Ross demanded of the navigation officer whose fingers were dancing deftly over the controls. She frowned worriedly at the large screen in front of her. Fenny, petite and frail at first glance, was nothing but. Ross had seen her in action over the last month, and she was hands down the best navigator he had ever met. That she took more than a second to answer him clearly indicated that something far from the ordinary had happened.

"The iffin SLH threw us out, Ross," Fenny informed. Running her fingers through her bushy mane, she swiveled around to look at Ross. Her charcoal-black eyes looked even darker than usual. "The inductive barriers collapsed and we dropped out of it like a boulder. We're in Sector 22. And that"—Fenny pointed at the predominantly orange orb next to them— "is the fourth planet in the Kyo-Sedra star system. This is iffin middle of nowhere."

This is nothing short of bizarre, Ross thought. Discovered two centuries ago, the Super Luminal Highways were wormhole networks built for spacecrafts traveling across galaxies using the faster-than-light Nongbut drives. The existence of the Confederacy was made possible largely due to the SLH, and their maintenance was the Confederacy's top priority. Ross had never heard of such sudden collapse of inductive barriers that made sure traffic stayed within the corridor, and seeing how high Fenny's eyebrows had shot up, Ross deduced that she hadn't heard of anything like it either.

"How far are we from the next AP?" he asked.

An AP, or access point, was the only place to get back on the SLH. But there was a problem: while outside the highway, the *Endeavor* couldn't use its faster-than-light a.k.a. Super Luminal mode. In ordinary mode, even if the *Endeavor* was retrofitted with a state-of-the-art depleted delmidium ore engine and extra thrusters, it'd take considerable time to reach the AP.

"It's near the second planet. Thirty pulses, fifty-one hours," Fenny said quickly.

"Damn!" Ross got off his chair and stared a while at Fenny's screen. It was ablaze with the bright orange planet; the twin stars of the system peeked from beyond it. "Take us there as fast as you can, Wiz," he said.

Wiz, the stocky pilot with long, well-groomed sideburns, responded with a flamboyant salute.

"Damn!" Ross cursed again. This was more complicated than he had thought. It meant significant impact on their plans. And that in turn meant he had to inform the captain right away. It was protocol. But Captain Terenze Milos had finished his shift at the COM barely an hour ago, and anyone who knew the man knew he didn't like to be awakened untimely from his sleep.

Ross shifted uneasily on his feet. Had it been anyone else, Ross wouldn't have hesitated as much, but Terenze Milos was a legend. In the long war of Locusta-Vanga that solidified the position of the Galactic Confederacy, Captain Milos was a hero. Post-war, Captain Milos didn't rest on his laurels; he'd practically walked away from them. Why? No one knew. Even though Ross had never found Captain Milos any less than affable — one could say he was unexpectedly lax for a man with his experience and background — nervous jitters always engulfed Ross's gut when he was in the presence of the captain. The fact that Ross was the newest addition to *Endeavor's* five-member crew and proving his worth to the captain was on the top of his agenda didn't help much either.

Ross drew a breath to compose himself before he buzzed the captain.

"About time, Commander," Captain Milos said in a gruff voice. The captain had been expecting him, Ross realized. He had likely been awakened by the alarm, yet he hadn't tried to find out what was going on. Ross suppressed a sigh. This was another peculiar thing about the captain—he'd push the crew into handling iffy situations with little oversight, sometimes to an extent that someone would think he didn't care. But Ross knew far too well that wasn't true. He chalked it up to the captain's way of assessing his crew's strength or perhaps a tactic to toughen them up.

"Why are we outside the SLH?" the captain demanded.

Ross explained as quickly as he could. In return, Captain Milos made an odd guttural sound. "I don't like this," the captain said.

Ross sympathized. This addition of fifty-one hours would make them late at Komilah. The Komilahn traders who had paid for the Pterostrich eggs wouldn't be happy.

"I'm sure the Komilahns will understand, Captain," Ross said. "It's not like we're late every time."

In fact, the *Endeavor* was never late. Terenze Milos had gone from being a celebrated captain of the Confederate Space Fleet to owner of a freight ship, but he ran his freight operations just like he had run his military command. "If you aren't an hour early, you're late," he always said, and his customers never had any reason to be unhappy.

Captain Milos grunted and Ross wondered what it could mean. He guessed that the Komilahns were not what worried the captain. He was probably worried about being dropped out of the SLH. Or could it be something else altogether?

A sharp beep jolted Ross out of his thoughts. The comm on the captain's seat was the source of the noise. Ross walked over, pressed the largest button, and a woman's voice that was soft, graceful, yet exuding command, streamed in. "Terenze? I need to see you right away. I've got something to show you."

"Sosa, the captain's off-shift, but I'll tell him."

"Yes, please do that," Sosa replied.

Sosa, the ship's enigmatic medic, was the only person Ross knew of who called the captain by his first name. She was also the only one on board who didn't engage in the observance of a military chain of command on the *Endeavor*.

"This is a freight ship, Terenze, not a military battleship," Sosa had told the captain many times. "You may always be the captain, but the rest of us are just regular people. No one's a lieutenant here, or an ensign. Try calling people by their names."

Perhaps it was hard for the captain to let go of his years of habit, or perhaps he saw a benefit to making his crew pretend they were part of a military command. Whatever the reason, Captain Terenze Milos wasn't about to completely change his ways. And Ross was happy that he didn't. Too young to enlist during the Locusta-Vanga war, Ross had attempted joining the Confederate Space Fleet post-war, but he was rejected all three times he tried. The fleet's physical training was simply too rigorous to withstand. So when Ross chanced a spot on the *Endeavor* as the captain's chief, it was the next best way of realizing his lifelong dream of serving in a military command. Perhaps, Ross thought, with Captain Milos on the *Endeavor*, it was even better than being in the Space Fleet.

Turning off the central comm, Ross turned to his personal wrist-mounted communicator. "Captain, that was Sosa. She needs to see you right away."

"All right," the captain replied. "I'll join you at the COM shortly. Just steer us toward the AP."

"Yes, Captain," Ross replied, even though he badly wished Captain Milos could be at the COM that very second, but that did not seem likely. The captain heeded most of Sosa's dictums with utmost earnestness. Like now. Ross wondered what Sosa needed to show the captain so urgently. Regardless of the reason, Ross had to handle COM and this weird turn of events on his own.

"Thank you, Commander," the captain said before a sharp click cut off the channel.

Ross drew a long breath. This was the third time the captain had referred to his as "commander." He had used the term once when Ross was hired a month ago and the second time when the *Endeavor* had been attacked by the Swarm, a nasty bunch of space pirates in

Sector 79.

Something about this situation has spooked the captain, Ross thought as he walked over to Fenny's side. Her screen was still lit up by the mighty orange planet.

"Fenny, can you get me a read of the system?" Ross said.

"Right away," Fenny replied. After a few clicks, her screen split into four, showing feed from scopes from all around the *Endeavor*. The orange planet, whose basic Confederacy name was Kyo-Sedra-4, hogged the top-right screen, but the others showed the areas of the Kyo-Sedra system that stretched behind the *Endeavor* and to the sides.

"Behind us is Kyo-Sedra-6," Fenny informed, pointing at a large blue striated planet behind them. "An ice giant," she added, but Ross's eye was drawn to a large flash on another screen that showed an area left of the *Endeavor*.

"What the heck was that?"

"What in the—"

With a couple of taps, the feed from the ship's left scope filled the screen. It showed a planet, white and shiny, a distance away from the *Endeavor*. Its view through the scope quickly turned grainy as Fenny maximized the enlargement.

"That is"—Fenny looked up her star charts—"Kyo-Sedra-5. But something's wrong with that iffin planet. It's not supposed to have space rocks floating around it."

Yet there it was, a field of shiny specks all around the circumference of the planet.

"Holy God of the stars," Fenny exclaimed loudly. "Do you see that, Ross?"

He saw it clearly. A large blob of black swirled on the lower left half of Kyo-Sedra-5.

"Something crashed into KS-5? An asteroid? Perhaps part of it broke up above KS-5 and—"

"No, I don't think so," Ross said. Even though he could not believe what he was about to say, he went on. "That's no asteroid remains. I think that's a debris field. Someone just eviscerated a space fleet."

"Sorry, Ross, but it can't be," Wiz chimed in. "Never heard of a space fleet in this sector. There's no record of one in the charts either."

"I know fleet debris when I see one," Ross said, ignoring Fenny's doubtful look. He was an energetic fifteen-year-old when the Locusta-Vanga war had broken out. Too young to be part of the fleet, Ross had applied for a position as a recon specialist. The Confederacy wanted to bring all its lost soldiers home, and Ross and many other youngsters learned to pick up remnants of lost fleets from distant views just like this. Ross had found a way to be useful to the cause, but learning firsthand the cost of a galactic battle eventually took its toll on him.

"So . . ." Fenny asked hesitantly. "What do we do about it?"

"Analyze the debris. Once you have confirmation, we need to report to the Confederacy. Also run a scan for life."

Ross walked over to the captain's seat and slid into it, wincing at the cold, unwelcoming surface under him. There would be no survivors, he knew that well. But that was not what sat like a mountain on his mind. The bigger question was what could have caused the destruction. And what was a fleet doing here? His finger hovered on the button of his comm port. Was it too soon to get the captain on board?

"Ross." Fenny's sharp voice cut through the tightness of the room. "I read a beacon. It's asking for help."

That was impossible. No one could live through a catastrophe like this. Or was it a miracle, one that he had been hoping for all through the Locusta-Vanga war but never found?

Wiz swiveled around to face Ross. "What now?"

There was no question, not in his mind anyway.

"Change course, Wiz. We're going to KS-5 to check for survivors."

Wiz didn't turn around as quickly as he usually did when receiving an order. Instead, his eyes narrowed. That was expected, Ross admitted grudgingly to himself. They were late on the Komilahn run and Captain Milos had asked to set the course for the AP himself. Besides, this situation was weird and unnerving on the whole. Something didn't quite fit.

Hell, nothing fit.

But however bad a situation he might be leading the *Endeavor* into, Ross couldn't ignore a call for help. Not in a million years, not ever. And he also knew Captain Milos would agree.

"That's an order, Wiz," Ross said, burying his doubts under a veneer of calm. "Take us to KS-5. I'll brief the captain."

"One good turn is worth doing well."

— Mwandan proverb

1

Ramya Kiroff swerved to one side to dodge the blade that came swinging at her, but it still grazed her arm, making the alarm fashioned into her training suit emit an annoying, high-pitched hum.

"Kiroff," Istapol Maroni, the Institute's top trainer who was well known for his dogged penchant for discipline, shouted. "Focus."

Ramya steadied herself and gripping her sword tighter, returned her opponent's blow. Her peer, Armand Danukis, the favored cadet of their year, parried effortlessly and smirked.

"Is there anything you're good at, Kiroff?" Armand jeered, his hazel eyes glinting with ridicule through the steel mesh of his face mask. "Anything at all?"

You'll see, Danukis. I'll shut you up for good this time. Ramya brought down her sword in a slicing motion across Armand's combat-suit clad torso, but he stopped it midway, his own blade set firmly between her sword and his chest.

His brows danced. "That's the best you can do? Hasn't your father taught you anything? They say he's the greatest swordsman in Raonic times."

He was indeed. Her father was also the richest man in Raonic times . . . and the most heartless father Ramya could've had.

"He must be so proud of you, Kiroff," Armand said, tossing his dark curls and chuckling. "Heiress to his empire can't win a duel to save her life."

Ramya stiffened. This was not something she wanted or needed to hear. She didn't need reminding of her father's disappointment in her, especially not when she needed to win this duel so desperately.

"Trysten Kiroff's luck sure ran out with you," Armand scoffed. "His firstborn, not only a girl, but also one as useless as you."

Shut up!

Armand wasn't far from the truth though. Trysten Kiroff, her father, owner of a fiefdom that included five mineral-soaked planets over three star systems, never would've wanted a daughter. At least not a firstborn who by the Confederacy's laws of inheritance would be the sole legal heir to the house.

Armand bared his impossibly perfect set of teeth. "He must wish you dead so your baby brother can be his heir instead."

I won't let you inside my head.

She struck a straight jab at his torso, but he blocked it right away. The jab was a calculated move, because she knew what he would come with next.

Come on, step back and try your favorite swipe.

Ramya smiled as Armand took a step back and raised his arm just like she had expected. She waited until the last moment before ducking to avoid the sweep, expecting to catch Armand by surprise. Her calculations were correct. He momentarily lost his balance and stumbled forward. Whirling around to face his back, Ramya thrust her blade with full force into his suit, right where his heart would be.

The tip of her blade flashed red at contact, and electronic messages relaying the kill strike spread to the monitoring units. A shrill alarm blasted across the arena.

Gotcha!

At the sound of clapping, Ramya took her eyes off the crouching Armand Danukis and glanced at the stands ringing the spacious dueling arena. It had been near empty to begin with and it was still sparse now. Except for the trainer Maroni, who had burst into applause, there were three others who had come to cheer on Armand. They now sat with drooping faces. In addition, there was an unintroduced visitor in a dark blue coat who sat a distance away from Armand's pals.

Maroni held up a baton that glowed white, signaling the end of the duel. "Win to Kiroff," he announced as he headed toward the ring.

Armand rose to his feet and glowered. "A strike from the back, eh?" he said, baring his teeth in a vicious scowl. "Just what is expected from one of your house, come to think of it. You hearth-less vagrant insects are best at sneaking your way into other people's territories when their backs are turned."

"I won fair and square, Danukis," Ramya spat. While she cared little about the house that had never really respected her, an outsider—especially someone from a rival house like Danukis— calling her family names made her insides bristle.

As with every Kiroff before her, being called "hearth-less" particularly stung. When the galaxy was settled hundreds of years ago, every noble family was given a piece of land where they built their hearth, erected their homes, and raised their families. Hearths were a family's lifeline, an inheritance to be protected with life. Back in those days, when enmity and competition between houses wasn't about wresting business deals from each other under cover of apparent civility, disputes often ended in usurping an enemy's hearth. A hearth-less family was a refugee with no land to call their own, their nobility stripped off along with the lost land, their position reduced to bottom of societal approval. House Kiroff was unfortunate enough to lose their hearth.

Callen Moanu, Ramya repeated the name in her mind, the name of the man who had snatched the Kiroff hearth, the name etched in the memory of every Kiroff since. Although it had happened a long time ago, and although the Kiroffs had re-built their fortunes and re-established themselves in galactic society once again, the original stigma remained fresh, thanks to people like Armand Danukis.

"Quite like your father after all," Armand went on as he pulled his protective headgear off. "He won the Carboni contracts just as fairly, last year and every year before that. He also won your mother's hand honorably, didn't he? Too bad the whore birthed a loser like you."

In all her seventeen years, Ramya had not known love of a

mother. Nurses, governesses, boarding schools it had been, the mother Armand just called a whore was no more than Lady Sonya Kiroff to her, a dusky beauty and famous socialite whose demeanor turned icy whenever Ramya was near. All her life, Ramya had longed for her affection, and then learned to hate her with fervor. Yet, Armand's insult lit a fire in her head in an instant. Her fists curled into balls and without a second thought, she swung as hard as she could and slammed her fist into Armand's jaw making him teeter and fall to the shimmery mosaicked floor. Pain shot through Ramya's hand and she winced, but the pain was worth it.

"Kiroff," shouted Maroni. He crossed the distance between the stands and the ring with long, powerful strides. "Stand down."

Boos rose from the stands. *Danukis's stupid posse*, Ramya thought as she rubbed her hand.

Maroni rushed over, grabbed her by the arm, and swung her around. "This is disgraceful, Kiroff," he snapped. "Did you forget we have a visitor today?"

Ramya stole a glance. The visitor, the white-haired man in blue with eyes to match, stood with his arms crossed. Behind him, Armand's cronies were still booing to their heart's content.

"Stand up, Danukis." Maroni stepped toward Armand. "Let's look at you."

Armand was lying on the ground, balled up like an armadillo. What in the stars was he doing that for? It was just one punch. It couldn't have done more than leave a bruise on his fat jaw.

Her heart froze when Armand rose to his feet with a grunt. His gloved hands were clamped over his mouth and nose, and drops of blood trickled through his fingers and onto his combat suit.

Not blood! Drawing blood was never good. That was a sure enough reason to be called to the administrator's office.

Maroni pressed a button on the talker clamped to his belt. "Send Medaid to Arena 4."

"You bitch," Armand hissed, and Ramya's fists curled once more.

Armand took a step forward but stopped when more blood trickled down the front of his suit, staining the front of it brown.

"Danukis," Maroni warned. "Watch your conduct or I'll have to send you to the admin's office."

"Why?" Armand's charcoal black eyes flashed. "Just because she's the heiress of House Kiroff she gets a pass after wounding me like . . . this and you hold a simple word against me?"

Ramya didn't hesitate to shout back. "'Bitch' is a simple word now? You uncivilized lout."

Maroni held his arms up. "Stop! No one is getting a pass," he informed. Ramya felt her trainer's watery brown eyes rest briefly on her, but she didn't care to meet his gaze. She knew his bushy brows would be pulled into a knot and his lips stretched into lines. A decorated veteran of the Locusta-Vanga war, Maroni was as rigid about honorable conduct as he might have been during his time in the forces. He was clearly outraged, but his anger was the least of Ramya's worries. The real trouble was facing the admin.

"She should be expelled from the Institute," Armand said.

Right. Like I've killed you or something. Regardless of the frivolity of her offense or its justification, she'd be punished. No doubt about that. She had drawn blood during training, after the duel was called, and in presence of a visitor. She was going to be suspended for sure. At least for a week.

A pair of white-clad medics rushed in and Maroni clicked his heels at Ramya. "Let's go, Kiroff."

He gently but forcefully pushed her along. They stepped off the stone floor of the arena and strode along the paved walkway that cut through the lush lawns of the Commerce, Administration, and Warcraft Strategy Institute, or CAWStrat, as it was known across the galactic colonies.

"You're taking me to the admin?" she asked as she and Maroni walked down the white-marbled corridors of the institute.

Maroni's jaws tightened. "Do you expect to go unpunished after that shameful conduct?"

Ramya breathed in deep. Of course she didn't, but her outburst was not without reason.

"Armand insulted my house, my mother," she said, hoping Maroni would reconsider. "I couldn't just take it—"

"A true statesperson knows better than to react to random slurs, Kiroff," Maroni cut her off, his voice tight. "After two years at the CAWStrat, you should know that. Have you been paying heed to anything we've been teaching you?"

She should've controlled her temper better. But that was easier said than done. Particularly with Armand, whose history with her family went back generations, as did the hostility. For more than a century, House Danukis had competed with House Kiroff over political, social, and financial influence across the galaxy, but they had never been able to outmaneuver the Kiroffs. The Danukis' jealousy was not unwarranted and Armand's animosity toward her not unexpected.

Maroni's steps slowed as the duo neared the double vaulted doors of the administrator's office. Ramya kept her gaze away from the impressive but intimidating dark-amber wood panels. She'd seen them far too many times, and none of the previous visits had left pleasant memories.

Please, God of the stars, let Leona be in a good mood. Leona Calibe, the administrator of the CAWStrat in charge of student activities, was hardly ever in a good mood.

"Ready, Kiroff?" Maroni paused a moment at the door. The trainer's gaze had softened, but his sympathies were useless when facing Leona.

Two assistants were buzzing around the silver-haired administrator when Maroni led Ramya into the sprawling chamber. Leona, clad in a white coat that was tailored to fit her slender, gaunt figure, was staring out the windows that overlooked CAWStrat's perfectly manicured lawns, her whiteness in stark contrast to the rest of the room decorated in swaths of dark colors. Leona dismissed her assistants with a careless wave of her hand as soon as the visitors were announced.

"Hello, Lady Ramya." Her voice was as glacial as those pale blue eyes. "We meet again."

Ramya forced a curt smile. They had met two days ago and a week before that, both times because Ramya had protested against the fission capsules they used in the fuel unit of the training scramjets. While running a scan on the jets, she had found a weakness in its protective sheath. In normal mode, it was perfectly safe, but it could cause a catastrophe during a crash. The CAWStrat and Leona had refused to see the issue.

"Drawn blood after the duel was called? That's reaching for the bottom."

The news had reached her already. Not unexpected. The medics would've filed a report in the time it took for Ramya and Maroni to cross the arena and find their way in Leona's office.

"Even the presence of a visitor from the GSO didn't deter you much, I see."

GSO? Ramya tried hard not to frown. The Galactic Special Ops was the premiere defense agency of the Galactic Confederacy, where most students of the CAWStrat hoped to score an internship. It was odd though that someone from the GSO would be observing a duel between juniors at the CAWStrat.

Never mind that, Rami. Focus!

Ramya pushed the nagging questions away. Right now she had to get out of Leona's clutches . . . if she could.

"Perhaps you ought to ask me why I was outraged?" Ramya said.

Leona's mouth fell open for a second and then she closed it forcefully, which Ramya thought resembled a crocodile's jaws clamping over hapless prey. Next to Ramya, Maroni shifted on his feet.

"Should I now?" Leona snapped.

Her excuse hadn't worked with Maroni, and there was little chance it'd work with Leona, but she had to try. "Armand Danukis besmirched my house, my mother."

A smile twisted Leona's lips. "What Armand Danukis said is not the matter of this meeting. What we—"

"How can you say that?" Ramya blurted. "What he said is the reason—"

"Insolence! Seems like you're intent on being a rebel instead of the statesperson we hope to make you," Leona said. "Hardly the deportment of an heiress, and certainly not fitting the house you come from. You are nothing like the triumph this institute had in your father."

Some people just couldn't help bringing up her father. The comparison wasn't new though, her father had seen to that. Yet, it made her cringe every time.

"I shudder to think of the possibilities," Leona continued in a bristling monotone. "You seem like a lost cause. Reminds me of the disappointment I had in Lord Brynden."

Her father's youngest brother was the dark sheep of the family. Just like Ramya, Brynden wasn't "winner material." While his two brothers excelled and thrived, it was said that Brynden had been swallowed by the prohibited dark arts while at the CAWStrat. Before he could graduate at eighteen with honors like his two brothers before him, Brynden had simply vanished. Ten years had passed, and no one had heard from the missing Kiroff. Rumor had it that Brynden had become an overlord at the Fringe—a bunch of quasi-autonomous star systems at the northern outskirts of Confederacy space.

"Lord Brynden was always trouble. None of the brilliance one could expect of a great house. Now you, just like him." Leona grated to a halt and glared, her stubborn chin pointing accusingly at Ramya.

Maroni cleared his throat. "Armand Danukis was not exactly—" He stopped abruptly as Leona raised her hand.

"That'll be all, Trainer Maroni," Leona said. "You may leave us now. I shall discuss this incident with you in a separate sitting."

As soon as Maroni left the room, Leona beckoned Ramya to the side of the room away from the windows. The pit of Ramya's stomach dropped in an instant. *Not the summoning! Please don't call my father.*

Leona stopped at the darkest corner of her room where a small pedestal with a white ball on top was the only piece of furniture.

"Since this makes for one too many transgressions on your account, I had no choice left but to summon your father," Administrator Leona announced icily. "Please step inside. Just so you know, scowling highlights your poor conduct even more." As Leona puttered away to turn on the equipment, Ramya glared at her back.

As if it mattered to her father if she scowled. He couldn't stand her anyway. He never had. In his words, she was not "winner material" and Trysten Kiroff only liked to win.

Ramya remembered the incident on her tenth birthday, a day that was considered special for a girl. Trysten Kiroff had thrown the banquet of the century that was still talked about to this day. The gala had gone on for a week, and Somenvaar—the Kiroff family home—was lit up so bright that it could be seen all the way from Alle. Among the million gifts her parents had showered on Ramya, her favorite had been the chestnut pony her father had picked for her. For once Ramya had thought he cared. In her excitement, she had tried to scramble up the horse. She couldn't make it to the top, but fell instead, slamming into the hard ground.

Her father had laughed with the guests and causally walked over to her side. Ramya had noticed the anger burning in his pale-gray eyes as he towered over her.

"All my firstborn and the heiress of this magnificent house can do is make a spectacle of herself and make me hang my head in shame," her father spat through gritted teeth.

"I'm sorry," she had whispered, trembling like a leaf, wanting to melt into the ground.

"Take the horse away," her father had ordered a servant.

"Destroy it. I don't want to see it ever again."

"Father," Ramya had dared to call him pleadingly.

His eyes were stones when he looked at her. "You should know. I can't tolerate seeing things that embarrass me. You're lucky you happen to have my blood in you."

It had been a birthday to remember.

"Lady Ramya, stand tall," Leona's sharp voice cut through the fog of memories and hit Ramya like a whip. She stiffened and holding herself as erect as she could, turned toward the pedestal.

Leona had powered up the communication channels and a second or two later, the white ball lit up, forming the projection of a room above it. A man, dark-haired with mirthless, pale gray eyes stared out at them from the vaporous projection.

"Lord Paramount Kiroff, my greetings," Leona addressed Trysten Kiroff, placing her palms over her heart, five fingers outspread in a manner appropriate for greeting the head of a great house. Ramya's father simply nodded halfheartedly, his annoyed gaze skimming over Ramya before returning to Leona once more.

"Greetings, Leona," he replied, his voice as cold and dour as his gaze. "I have your report."

Ramya stiffened, her gut twisting into a tight knot. The witch had sent a report on the dueling incident already? She scrutinized her father's pale face, trying to assess the depth of his anger.

"It's a series of lamentable misconducts, Lord Kiroff," Leona said. "Far too many to ignore any longer, I'm afraid to say."

Ramya didn't miss Leona's nervous gulp when she paused. Just like everyone else, the administrator was afraid of Trysten Kiroff. He was rumored to be ruthless in his business dealings, and Ramya knew he could be cold. No one dared cross him or his house.

"Lady Ramya went berserk at her duel with Armand Danukis this morning," Leona stated.

Berserk? Really? Ramya stole a glance at her father. Was that a quiver in his brow?

"After the duel was called, she—"

"Your report has enough of that information, Leona," her father interrupted. "I assume you've requested this meeting for more than simply restating the facts. Am I mistaken?"

"Um, no, you are not, Lord Paramount Kiroff," Leona replied. "I wanted to inform you in person that we will have to suspend your daughter for a month."

A month? The witch had to be joking!

A telltale frown rippled across her father's forehead. "We?"

"The council of administrators, of course."

Her father sat back and tapped his chin thoughtfully. "In the ten minutes that have passed since the incident, you've had time to call a council, decide on a punishment, and then request a meeting with me. That's impressive. Seems to me you're determined, quite immensely so, to bring my daughter to justice."

Leona shifted on her feet and her jaw tightened. Ramya held back a snicker with every bit of willpower she possessed.

Leona's voice trembled as she replied, "Thank you, Lord Paramount. Those words of praise mean a lot coming from you. This afternoon we shall send your daughter home for her suspension."

"No, you won't."

Silence, taut and bristly, fell over the dark corner for a second or two. Then Leona squawked.

"You don't understand. I did not intend to discuss the situation but only to inform you of our decision."

"I understand your intent," her father replied, impatience making his words speed up. "But this is what needs to happen. You shall revise your decision and decide on a lesser sentence. Have her assist you after instruction hours, for instance."

"But—"

"I'm a busy person, Leona. And right now, I'm pondering the proposal you sent last week for modernizing the CAWStrat's space dome." Her father held up a binder emblazoned with the CAWStrat logo. "You wouldn't want me to be distracted while I'm working on that, would you?"

Let's see you combat that, witch! For the first time in a long time, Ramya felt the warm flood of happiness inside her. A parent's support was good to have when your back was against the wall. And if that parent happened to be Trysten Kiroff, there could be nothing better in the galaxy. But . . . Ramya reminded herself sternly, her father was only doing this to protect his image, not her.

"But, Lord Paramount Kiroff, we can't do that," Leona protested, her stout voice dwindling steadily into a whine. "That will be setting a dangerous precedent. The CAWStrat has always been above galactic power play. If we do this—"

"The CAWStrat has never been above anything, Leona. You know that well. Besides, I'm not saying my daughter should go unpunished for her . . . lapses, but I shall mete out the penalty myself. I give you my word."

Ramya's heart sank into an abyss. She had been hoping for a respite from Leona, but this was not the kind she wanted. Passing from Leona's hand into her father's was the proverbial jumping from the stewing pot into the fire. At least Leona's punishment would have been impersonal, but her father's . . . . She suddenly hoped Leona would resist the elder Kiroff's offer.

"I'm not sure I can—"

"Of course you can. And before I forget, I quite like the proposal for the space dome. House Kiroff is considering voting in favor of disbursing the funds you requested." Her father smiled. "There isn't anything else to discuss, I hope?"

Leona blinked a few times, and then shook her head. "No, nothing else at all." Leona placed her hand, fingers outspread, over her heart. "Apologies for taking up your time, Lord Paramount Kiroff. Good tidings to you."

A shadow of a smile floated over her father's face. "Good tidings, Leona."

He glanced at Ramya next, his icy gaze sweeping over her and soaking her heart with the fear of impending doom. "We shall speak shortly," was all he said to her before the projection went off air.

2

Trysten Kiroff, it was said, had the golden touch. Since he assumed leadership of House Kiroff from his father Lord Abelei, there was nothing stopping the family's rise. During his time, the Kiroffs' mining empire sprawled further, profits soared, and Trysten's younger brother Lynden was elected to the High Council of the Galactic Confederacy. House Kiroff's influence in the Raonic times was not unchallenged, yet unparalleled to date.

Such influence translated to great expectations on the next generation. The heir of a great house couldn't avoid the limelight even if they descended from someone lesser than Trysten Kiroff, but Ramya was sure her position was the worst. Being a female firstborn to a leader of a great house didn't help Ramya any. While the Confederacy didn't distinguish between males and females when it came to inheritance laws—the firstborn of a firstborn would carry the lineage, the Law of Bequests stated simply—a woman head of house was unusual and, like Ramya, faced greater scrutiny and carried a larger burden.

However, after the mishap at the duel with Armand Danukis, Ramya realized the benefits of her status. She had expected Administrator Leona to carry a grudge against her after her father coerced her to drop the sentence. But no, Leona acted as if the incident had never happened. She called Ramya to assist her after instruction hours, but was hardly her reproachful self. Armand and his minions stayed out of Ramya's way for the most part, and Ramya deduced that also had something to do with her father's cautioning.

Three days after the incident, Ramya sat in CAWStrat's main lunchroom with her best friend Isbet, eating, talking, and watching boys. Isbet did most of the talking and watching while Ramya stared out the tall glass walls. Magnificent mountains surrounded them, like sentinels watching over Confederacy Peak on which the pink CAWStrat buildings shone like a jeweled tiara.

"Come on, Rownack, just ask me already," Isbet muttered. She sat across the table from Ramya, twirling her curly locks around her finger as she poked absentmindedly at her food. Her eyes flitted back and forth between Ramya and the table directly on the opposite side of the corridor where two boys—both two years senior to them—were seated.

Isbet leaned across the table, frowned, and whispered, "By the God of the stars, girl, what do you keep staring at? It's like you're seeing the Tajita Ranges for the first time. And why do you keep frowning? Don't tell me you're still worried about that stupid duel with that idiot Armand?"

Ramya was worried. She had to be. Her father had said he'd speak to her. That was three days ago. She was still waiting for his summons.

Trysten Kiroff always kept his word. If he had promised Leona he'd take his daughter to task for her conduct at the duel, he was not about to let it slip. What in the stars was taking so long?

"Come on, Rami." Isbet reached over the table and tugged at Ramya's hand. "Forget about it. Move on. No one is talking about it— not Leona, or Armand, or those goofs who follow him around. Why can't you?"

Because my father hasn't. And until I know what punishment he's about to throw at me, I can't move on.

She shrugged at Isbet and decided to change the subject. "What's with Rownack? Still nothing?"

Isbet had been waiting for Rownack, a flight-honor-badged senior, who was seated at the table across the aisle, to ask her to the annual Concert Night event at the CAWStrat. She had turned down offers from two other boys in hopes that Rownack would ask her, but so far he had showed little interest in the matter. With only two days left until the event, Isbet was all nerves.

"Something's wrong with that guy," Isbet announced with a wave of her hand. "It's my mistake. Should've accepted when Arren asked. Now . . ."

"Why don't *you* ask Rownack instead?"

Isbet froze as if she had seen a ghost. Then blinking, she turned slowly to look at Ramya. "Me? Ask *him*? You gone mad, Rami?"

No! I just don't support your pigeonholing tendencies.

"The skies would part and the stars would rain fire on us if you did, hmm?" Ramya asked, not holding back the bite in her voice. A girl asking a boy out would be unconventional for sure, but how better to solve the tangle Isbet was in now?

Isbet made a face. "Not for you maybe," she said crossly. "You're the Kiroff heiress, the universe is in your palms. But if I asked a boy out, all hell would break loose."

Isbet was the fourth-born daughter of a second-born son from House Valpenrys, a lesser fiefdom under House Kiroff. From her low position in the hierarchy of power, the conventions of galactic social order seemed more binding. Ramya however thought it was just an excuse Isbet used, and her fear of hellfire from society was mostly fictional.

"Do what you will, Isbet," she said. "The other option is going to Concert Night without a partner. Now that sounds like more of a hell to me."

"Never mind my hell. What about you? Don't tell me you're going alone again?"

Ramya quickly suppressed a sigh. Isbet wouldn't understand. Since Ramya had turned fourteen and been debuted in social circles, boys had been flocking around her. Ramya was a generous mix of her parents' genes. Her oval face was framed by auburn hair that was rare among the Kiroffs and non-existent in Sonya's heritage, blue-gray eyes like her father's stood out in stark contrast on Sonya's dusky skin. Although Ramya was no great natural beauty like her mother, she was put together pleasingly. But then, even if she were ugly, she had more than enough to attract generous attention from the opposite sex—her social stature. Ramya Kiroff was considered a prize in the matrimonial market. Every boy she met was more interested in the riches she was set to come into rather than in her. Ramya hated it enough to stay away from the courting scene altogether.

"Rami? Hello? You didn't answer me," Isbet probed again.

"I told you already, Isbet," Ramya said. "I hate their empty praises, the show they put on to impress me."

"That's what boys do when courting girls," Isbet muttered between mouthfuls of julienned vegetables. "Would you rather they shout obscenities at you?"

"You know that's not what I meant. I'm invisible to them, Isbet. If I were a wall inheriting the Kiroff name and fortune, they'd sing my praises just as devotedly. What they really want, what they're really courting, is House Kiroff."

Isbet was not one to give up easily. She simply shrugged. "Well, at least they'll stay loyal even when you don't look half as good as you do now. That's not bad."

Why did she even argue with Isbet? "You're right," Ramya huffed. "Maybe you should send out word that Ramya Kiroff is looking for a partner. Perhaps we could set up a jousting tournament to pick a winner. I'm sure that'll make Leona pleased with me once again."

Isbet shook her curls and held her hands up in mock submission. "I get it, you're not interested. All right, forget boys," she said. Leaning forward, her eyes sparkling, Isbet whispered, "I heard some fresh rumor about the GSO today."

Now this was why Ramya endured Isbet's endless lectures on relationships. Being friends with Isbet had its perks; her immense network of informants served endless news and gossip, even though it required hearing about boys and advice on courtship nonstop.

"Tell me."

"So, there was a GSO agent at your duel, right? Guess what? He wasn't the only one around. There were many more around the CAWStrat. They came to the sessions, dropped by the arenas, and some simply walked the corridors."

That didn't make any sense. People from GSO — recruiters mostly — only showed up during the annual enlistment season which was still six months out. Even then, the recruiters didn't just stop by random places at the CAWStrat, not like this.

"What in the stars is going on? Are they here to watch over someone at the CAWStrat?"

Isbet shrugged and deftly munched on a piece of carrot.

"Or maybe they're here to guard something valuable. I've heard they keep a lot of defense-related . . . things . . . strategic plans, blueprints here," Ramya mused.

"No, not that."

"What then?"

"They're recruiting," Isbet informed, flashing a telling glance before digging into a gelatin pudding.

That was absurd. The GSO didn't recruit so often and never directly from the CAWStrat. Graduates from the Institute were given internships at the GSO, some of which could stretch as long as five years, and only after completing the internship successfully were promising candidates offered a position.

"You mean hiring interns?" Ramya asked.

"No. I mean recruiting."

Ramya could only shake her head in disbelief. Perhaps Isbet's informant was wrong.

"The GSO is on an emergency recruitment spree," Isbet whispered. Her eyes widened. "The word is the GSO has lost an entire fleet near Sector 22. An *entire* fleet."

Ramya sat up, frowning. This was impossible news. A Confederacy fleet was no small thing, and GSO fleets were the biggest among all kinds of fleets in the Confederacy. Even the smallest of them had to have ten battlecruisers, each with a thousand jets and two or three thousand people on board. What could've wiped out such a behemoth? There wasn't even a war going on.

"How?" Ramya managed a whisper. Isbet shrugged. "What's in Sector 22? There isn't much, is there?"

"Two star systems. No colonies."

"What could've wiped out a whole fleet? Wait . . . what was a fleet doing in Sector 22 anyway? The GSO usually have their exercises in the outer colonies."

Isbet shrugged again. "Don't know. Everyone's going on about how catastrophic the loss is and how the GSO is ramping up its forces to make up for it."

"When did this happen?" Ramya asked on a sudden hunch.

"Last week apparently."

That was probably why her father never called. The GSO fleet was mostly manufactured in mega-factories owned by House Kiroff. Not just that, most of the ores used to build the spacecraft also came from Kiroff mines. If the GSO was rebuilding its lost fleet, then it would mean sudden and tremendous demand on production. House Kiroff, particularly her father, had to be busy. Could he have forgotten his promise to Leona?

Fat chance!

"Wish I knew how what skills they're looking for in people," Isbet said meditatively.

"You want to join a GSO fleet?"

"Of course. Donning the blue has always been my dream. I didn't bust my haunches getting that flight honor badge for nothing," Isbet said. The girl loved to fly and was great at it also. For two years straight, Isbet, with her flawless flight record, had wrangled the flight honor badge from her frustrated, mostly-male counterparts.

Ramya was not too bad a pilot herself, but not nearly good enough for the flight honor badge. In the two years at CAWStrat, she had accumulated quite a few flight credits to her name and held a steady spot near the upper-mid-level pilot rankings among the trainees. Since joining CAWStrat, Ramya had grown to like flying.

Liking to fly was one thing though, but joining the fleet? That was serious commitment. Being part of the fleet wasn't exactly leisurely business. Apart from the ten-year vow of celibacy, rigors of training, and risk of combat, it also meant living in space for long stretches. Sometimes, GSO fleet personnel didn't set foot on land in years.

Years in that never-ending darkness of space. For the love of stars, what a life! Ramya fought the shudder threatening to rise up her spine, but failed. It shook her, slightly, but enough to catch Isbet's eye.

Isbet flashed an understanding smile. "Thinking of space still gives you the jitters, huh?"

At least it was just the jitters now. Ramya searched for a spot on the Tajita Ranges to fix her gaze. A year ago, during their first space flight at CAWStrat, she had totally lost it. She had not feared space before that, but being out in that tiny scrambler jet, all alone in the darkness . . .

Leona had made quite a spectacle out of Ramya's nervous breakdown. Her father had visited at the infirmary. He didn't even inquire about her health. "In all of my CAWStrat years, the flight honor badge was mine," he'd said. Every word meant to bite, gnaw, and rip into Ramya's heart. "It's a pity *my* daughter needed a rescue mission to salvage her scramjet."

She had failed her father and her magnificent heritage yet another time. Her father had not wasted the opportunity to hit her where it hurt most. He had cut off her access to the Kiroff spaceship factories.

"Prove yourself worthy and then you can visit again," he had hissed before leaving the infirmary, knowing well how much she loved touring the production lines and hanging around the design labs, watching little parts and pieces fit together to make a spacecraft. Someday, she hoped, she'd be able to bring her own designs to life.

Ramya had tried hard to prove herself since. She worked at improving her pilot rankings, fought back her fear of space flight. But her father hadn't budged.

Tired of being refused access, Ramya had found other ways to get into the factories. She couldn't visit in person, her father saw to that, but he couldn't stop her from hacking the networks, could he? Right from her room at CAWStrat, Ramya kept tabs on the Kiroff shipyards. She knew every spacecraft they built, every weapon they installed, and every new tech they researched. To this day, her father didn't know.

"Rami!" Isbet's sharp voice nudged Ramya out of her thoughts. "Let's get out of here." Rownack and his friend had finished their lunch and Isbet nodded meaningfully at them.

Ramya was about to shake her head at Isbet when she noticed the liveried man at the entrance. Her insides crumbled. The man was wearing the unmistakable colors of House Kiroff — red and gold. His name escaped her, but she recognized the man nonetheless; he was her father's personal messenger.

This couldn't be good. Isbet's voice reached Ramya's ears, but she couldn't make out the words. All she saw was the man as he scanned the lunchroom, his sharp gaze settling on Ramya within a few seconds. Before she knew it, he was next to their table, bowing.

"Lady Ramya," he addressed her in a deep, almost guttural voice and retrieved an envelope from his liveried smock. "I have a letter from Lord Paramount Kiroff." Another bow later, he was gone.

Ramya sat frozen in her chair, staring at the letter from her father, dread making her heart leaden. In Raonic times, letters were reserved for carrying the most joyful of news and the most dreadful ones as well. Her father, Trysten Kiroff, had no joy to share with her.

He has dispatched my punishment.

How apt that it was delivered just the way her father served his adversaries news of his victories over them: signed, sealed, and delivered via personal courier? Ramya's fingers hovered over the blood-red seal with a mighty and thorny "K," unable to gather up enough courage to unleash the verdict inside.

3

The evening skies were stained a deep shade of purple when Ramya finished reading her father's letter for the tenth time. She put it away and shuddered, as if the paper was burning her fingers. For a second she simply stared at it, then scowling, she crumpled it and tossed it into the trash receptacle. With teeth clenched and fists curled, Ramya watched until the last bits of paper crumbled into ash within the translucent vessel.

I'm never going to be your bartering chip, Trysten Kiroff. I don't care if House Kiroff goes to hell.

Seventeen years of trying to live up to her father's impossible expectations was enough. Was it her fault that she was born a girl? Was it her fault that she wasn't as perfect as he was? Her education at CAWStrat had to be terminated forthwith, her father had written. According to him, a strategic marriage was the best way Ramya could serve House Kiroff.

This wasn't the first time she had heard of her father's plan to marry her off to a man of his choosing, a man who would come from a reputable family of considerable wealth and add to the Kiroffs' clout, a man he would then groom to run the Kiroff business empire. Over the years she had hoped to convince him otherwise. She'd hoped he'd groom her instead, treat her like a worthy successor. She had hoped he'd be impressed by her records at CAWStrat, by the model spacecrafts she designed year after year. But no, he hadn't paid any attention to those.

And now, forcing her into a marriage even before she could graduate from CAWStrat? No, she wasn't about to tolerate that. She had to find a way out, escape her father. As Ramya looked into the full-length gilded mirror across the room, steely eyes looked back.

Ramya's fists clenched.

Find someone else to use in your power games. You won't have me.

Ramya looked askance at the mirror again. Her face looked gaunt and paler than usual. Her eyes swept over the expansive suite that had been her home at CAWStrat for two years. The massive room was yet another privilege the Kiroff name had brought her, a privilege not many others at the Institute were granted. It was unfair that she had to think of running away from everything she was used to having. Didn't she have a right to her inheritance?

Ramya flinched at the thought. Was an inheritance worth a lifetime of scorn? *No, it can't be!* Could she survive without things that came so easily to her? *I have to.*

Ramya shifted uncomfortably in her seat. There was no easy path out of this. If she wanted respect from her father, she had to earn it. Prove to him once and for all that she was worthy. Show him that she was better than him.

There was one thing that Trysten Kiroff didn't have, one thing that he had wanted all his life—the original hearth of the Kiroffs that Callen Moanu usurped years ago. If she could . . . somehow . . . wrest it back from the Moanus . . .

Ramya sat up, studying her hardening face in the mirror. She could do it. She had to. All she needed to do was find Callen Moanu's heir and make him relinquish the right over the Kiroff hearth. If she could, no one could call them hearth-less vagrants anymore. Her father would have to acknowledge her as worthy. Yes, that was the only way to have it both—her father's respect and her inheritance.

But . . . the Fringe was a lawless land far, far away. And she had never traveled that far on her own. The Moanus were elusive targets. Chances were, she wasn't going to find Callen Moanu's heir quickly, and it was possible that she'd not succeed in wresting the Kiroff's original hearth back from them. What then?

Ramya breathed in deep and let the light evening air wash the fear away. She sat up and stared at her reflection across the room. Her frowning face stared back at her.

She had to do something. She just couldn't go along and marry a power-hungry conniver picked by her father. She had to get away. Her fists curled, nails dug into her palms painfully. The pain did good. It cleared her mind of fear and grounded her. Hope came surging back into her heart.

If Uncle Brynden could leave home and make a name for himself, so could she. If that meant braving a trip to the galactic frontier, so be it. That would be a million times better than being dragged into a marriage of convenience. All her life her father had belittled her, and if she agreed to this marriage, she'd have husband who'd sneer at her for the rest of her life. No, she couldn't live with that.

Ramya strode to the massive windows that framed the sprawling gardens of CAWStrat outside. Neatly trimmed hedges crisscrossed flawlessly manicured lawns, flowering plants and shapely trees grew at strategic intersections of the meandering walkways. An ache welled up inside Ramya and she tore her gaze away from the scenery, heaving. That was just how her life looked from the outside—perfect.

Ramya knew it was anything but. And she had to fix it before it was too late.

But how? She couldn't just walk out of CAWStrat. How could she escape her father then?

Ramya's fingers clenched over the window frame as a plan grew—slow and hesitant at first before it rushed along at a breakneck pace—in her mind. She was going to get out of here. Yes, there was a way.

If only she could get herself a couple more days at CAWStrat.

4

In her two years at the CAWStrat, Ramya had never been happier or more excited for Concert Night. Her eyes swept over her reflection in the mirror, lingering on the tiara and its shimmering jewels scattered in a graceful pattern. *The things the Kiroff fortune can buy*, Ramya mused. That tiara alone cost more than a year's tuition at the CAWStrat, an amount families of most cadets considered difficult to scrape together. For the Kiroffs though, an extravagant display of wealth on Concert Night was the natural way of doing things.

A sigh weaved its way out of Ramya as she thought of how she had begged her father to allow her to stay at the Institute for an additional week. She was almost down on her knees pleading him to reconsider his ultimatum.

"One more week, Father," she had implored. "Just one more week, please."

Ramya didn't need a week, only two days. But she had to play it safe. And for once, she got lucky. Trysten Kiroff relented. Perhaps he felt sorry for her. Perhaps he had just signed a mighty business deal and felt merciful. Who knew? Either way, it didn't matter what he felt or thought. All Ramya needed was permission to stay through Concert Night.

She glanced at the travel pack under her bed and the frown bunching her forehead faded immediately. A few more hours and she'd be gone. Far away from the maddening, suffocating world of the CAWStrat and her father's clutches. In a couple of days she'd reach the outer colonies and possibly the Fringe. Then she'd have to find Uncle Brynden or the heir of Callen Moanu. If luck sided with her, she'd find both. If . . .

Ramya stopped her thoughts before they sped out of control. *One step at a time*, she reminded herself. Finding Moanu's heir had to wait. First, she had to get off Nikoor, but there was another step before that, the biggest step: getting out of the CAWStrat.

Ramya pulled out the pack and checked its contents again. Money, fake pass, baton . . . she had everything. Concert Night would be the perfect cover for her getaway. It was a big event at the CAWStrat, and invited guests, hired hands — stewards, stewardesses, musicians, cooks, waiting staff — swarmed the Institute. With so many people streaming in and out of the gates, security was stretched thin. No one would notice if she posed as a stewardess and walked out.

The biggest exodus of the helpers took place right after the fifth and final dance — a long thirty-minute Decosset — of the night and before the banquet afterward. That was when she had to get out.

Ramya had just finished putting on her jewels — thankfully less extravagant than her yellow gown — when the door flew open. Isbet rushed in, sparkling like a sapphire.

"Rami, pick one," she said breathlessly, waving a pair of tiaras. She stopped abruptly and scanned Ramya. "Wow, they've outdone themselves this year." Noticing Ramya grimace and roll her eyes, she added, "You look beautiful, Rami."

Ramya glanced at herself in the mirror and winced at her Concert Night attire, an intricate affair of yellow silk and taffeta, embroidered with lavish sprinkles of precious metal, gemstone, and crystal beads. Her wardrobe was not her own choosing, never had been since her debut three years ago. Everything beyond her CAWStrat uniform was put together meticulously by House Kiroff's stylists. Ramya, her attire and deportment included, was a Kiroff family statement.

"As beautiful as a lemon cake," Ramya muttered.

Isbet broke into giggles. "You're grouchy. Perfect mood for concert night, just perfect."

Ramya drew a deep breath, busying herself in choosing a tiara for Isbet.

"You've been this way since you got the letter from your father,"

Isbet said. Her keen observant eyes were glued on Ramya's face. "I don't like this grouchy you. I miss my cheerful friend. She's gone. Please bring her back."

After tonight I'll really be gone. Away from this place, from my father and his expectations.

Ramya picked a tiara, placed it on Isbet's glossy curls and smiled. "This is perfect. Rownack will be at a loss for words."

"He better be. After all the trouble I went into asking him to Concert Night."

Ramya chuckled. Indeed! Isbet had shown her mettle for sure. As expected, there had been raised brows and reproachful snickers thrown her way, but the girl shrugged it all away.

"You seem ready. Let's go," Isbet said.

Ramya sighed. She was ready to go. "Wait a minute, Isbet," Ramya called when they were near the door. They had been best of friends for years, but Ramya was not one to display her emotions. Tonight was different though. She couldn't tell Isbet of her plans to run away, but sadness overwhelmed her at the thought of not seeing Isbet for a long time. Tears burned her eyes as Ramya threw her arms around Isbet's neck and held her.

Thank you for being my friend.

Isbet's eyes were wide even after Ramya had released her from the embrace. A look—puzzled, with a dash of worry—floated on Isbet's face. She was about to say something when the sound of laughter drifted in from the hallways beyond. Ramya used the distraction to tug Isbet's arm and led her out. "Let's go."

They were soon lost in a parade of colors, swishing, swirling in a careful rush toward the banquet hall, greeted by their companions and ushered into the lavish insides of the venue. The banquet hall was spectacular, with its brocaded walls of purple, blue, red, and gold, the looming chandeliers each the length of three grown men, and the intricate flooring a patchwork of black and white stone.

At Somenvaar—House Kiroff's ancestral abode and the largest

castle on planet Nikoor—Ramya had seen grander halls, and the banquet hall at the CAWStrat scarcely awed her on regular days. Things were different at Concert Night however. The hall was not simply a gaudy object of art meant to awe and impress, but a vessel brimming with joy and vigor. The gathering of youngsters was far smaller than the grand balls at Somenvaar, but the happiness in the room eclipsed that of any party her father had thrown.

However, there was no dearth of the sticky attention Ramya abhorred. Eyes, greetings, requests for a dance started pouring as soon as she stepped inside the banquet hall. A practiced smile pasted on her lips, Ramya made her calculations while a delighted, young CAWStrat senior escorted her to the first dance of the evening.

Three roundes, then a break during the fourth. Ramya wished she could avoid the final dance, but that'd draw too much attention. But even if she got back on the dance floor for the final rounde—the thirty-minute Decosset—she'd have to leave before it ended. She needed ten minutes to get to her room and prepare to mingle with the crowd of workers leaving the CAWStrat at the end of the dances. It would be tricky, leaving the hall during the Decosset without attracting attention. She had to manage it somehow. She had to get back to her room to change into plain street attire. Tonight was her best and only chance to get out of the CAWStrat and her father's diktats.

The fake pass worried her the most. *If that fails . . .* Ramya steeled herself. There was no reason the pass would be detected as a fake. CAWStrat cadets used such passes often to slip out of the Institute for a night outside. No one ever got caught.

Ramya hoped Isbet wouldn't mind that she stole her pass. There was no other way. That exit pass would let her past the gate check. She didn't know what access rights still existed on Isbet's pass, but if it had sufficient Lieres on it, that piece of plastic could secure Ramya's trip to the nearest space port off Nikoor.

God of the stars, bless me with some luck. The only other thing Ramya needed was money and she had more than enough of it. Yet again, being a Kiroff had helped.

Music ebbed and surged, and Ramya spent the entire time in a haze of thoughts. Her spirits rose and fell like the music — hope making it soar before worries weighed it down. She had not traveled off the planet much. She had visited the capital a few times, but that was only the next star system, aboard a luxury cruiser, surrounded by family and waited on by staff. Tonight, her first time traveling alone and in the guise of a commoner would be different.

I can do it. I have to.

"Having fun?" Isbet's voice made her jump. "Everything all right?" She peered at Ramya's face.

"Why not?" Ramya said, determined to not let Isbet pry too much or too deep. The fourth rounde was about to start, her time for a quick reconnaissance. If Isbet saw her sitting it out, she'd be suspicious as hell. "How's your dance? Rownack?"

Isbet beamed. "He's perfect. Best Concert Night ever."

"Good. I need a break before the final rounde," Ramya said, waving in the direction of the refreshment rooms, realizing her mistake in the last second. What if Isbet wanted to come with her?

"Do you want me to come with you?" Isbet offered.

Ramya hastened to pacify her. "No, no. I'll be fine. You carry on."

As soon as Isbet turned toward the dance floor, Ramya backed away. She pretended to walk to the refreshment rooms, but slipped behind the curtains when no one was looking. All she needed was a quiet place to catch her breath and collect her thoughts. In the hall, music surged. Gathering her flowing gown in her arms, Ramya weaved past the heavy brocaded drapes, counting doors.

She stopped at the fourth verandah and peered out the colossal glass doors that stood open to the sprawling grounds below. A draft blew in, chilly and refreshing. Ramya stood still for a moment, filling her lungs with the cold air, letting it calm her. CAWStrat's altitude and position in the northern coordinates of Nikoor meant a temperate climate all year around. It was hard to believe this was the middle of summer.

Somenvaar would be balmy now. The Kiroff estate was not far from here, but it was to the south and sat low, cradled by coastlines. Even Trysten Kiroff's frigid bearing couldn't keep Somenvaar cool this time of year. Chuckling under her breath, Ramya strode into the verandah.

"Watch out!"

The raspy yet almost melodic voice of caution leaped out from the darkness but a moment too late. She crashed, shoulder first into a man. The crystal goblet he was holding tipped, spilling its golden contents on him.

Damn it! Of course there had to be someone on the one verandah that she needed to herself.

"I thought CAWStrat cadets were trained in vigilance," the man said, brushing the dregs off his dark blue jacket, "and here you practically ran into a wall."

"Sorry," Ramya sputtered. She didn't care much about his snide evaluation of her skills, as her thoughts were elsewhere. She desperately needed some time to calm her senses, some quiet. Perhaps she could make the man leave? She parted the draperies a little. "The attendants at the refreshment room will be able to help you. Would you like to—"

To her dismay, the man waved away her suggestion. He leaned back on the balustrade, took a sip at what remained of his drink, and shook his head. "It's not much of a stain. Besides, I'm past being a cadet trying to win the attention of some winsome lass."

She snapped to attention. Why hadn't she noticed? He wasn't of the CAWStrat, neither a student nor staff. Ramya's eyes narrowed as she scanned the man's appearance. He was wearing the blues, the uniform of the GSO corps. He had to be older than a fresh graduate out of CAWStrat, but not by that much. In the dimly lit verandah, she couldn't tell the color of his closely cropped hair or eyes, only that they were both dark. His nose was a sharp presence on his angular face and his cheekbones were slightly raised. As she took in his features, the man's thin lips curled into a smile.

"Why are you missing out on a dance?" he said, appraising gaze sweeping over her. "You've obviously prepared well for tonight."

All she wanted was some quiet. Did the stars have to drop a nosey chipmunk on her instead?

Ignoring her silence, the man continued, "Putting together an ensemble like yours can't be easy. How do you find time to do that while being a CAWStrat cadet?"

He didn't know who she was. That was a good thing. Ramya flashed an ambiguous smile. "It's not that hard. We do it in groups," she replied, thinking of how Isbet pooled resources with other girls.

"I see," he said. There was something odd about the way he looked at her, a glint of disbelief in his eye perhaps? Ramya couldn't quite put a finger on it.

I should be thankful. At least he's not fawning over me like every other man.

"Why aren't *you* dancing?" she shot back, hoping to veer the conversation away.

He took another sip of his drink and smiled. "What's the point?"

"What do you mean?"

"It's all too senseless. I'm too old to stomach the useless waste of time anymore."

"You sound just like my grandmother," Ramya replied, smiling. "Doesn't seem like you're pushing seventy though."

He tilted his head and shot her a wise look. "I've spent close to a quarter century being alive. Well, almost. That's enough time to cultivate some cynicism in my veins, I think."

Ramya chuckled. Until now, she thought she was the only one to think of Concert Night in such cynical terms. She wasn't the one odd duck in the universe after all.

"Useless?" she asked regardless. "It's the one night cadets wait for all year long."

"I know. All you kids, pairing up like you've been matched up by the stars, as if you've deciphered your destiny. It's all a farce. How much of this do you think will last? Little." He paused and stared across the gardens toward the horizon. "Most of it is driftwood floating on an ocean of politics, power games, and strategic marriages. All this affection is waiting to be swept away in a heartbeat."

Didn't she know that? Her father was about to give her away just so his empire could grow some more.

The man went on, "Give it a few more years and you'll see — friends turned into bitter enemies over planetary rights, couples torn apart and sent to opposite ends of the galaxy perhaps never to meet each other again . . ."

She studied his face, not missing the hardened jaws and the gritted teeth. He had to have lost someone he loved. The music inside had died down, a few faint strains wafted in the air. Stillness tiptoed around them, interrupted only by a breeze or two.

"Perhaps you'll be married to your best friend's beau."

A picture Isbet and Rownack dancing together flashed before Ramya's eyes at his words and made her shudder. They, too, like every cadet at CAWStrat, would be swept away by galactic politics. The man was right. It was pointless. But Isbet was having the time of her life. Wasn't that worth something?

Sound of flutes rippled through the air and Ramya's muscles tightened. It was time to get back inside; the Decosset would soon begin. She was about to excuse herself when the man turned around.

"My apologies," he said. The sadness of moments ago had vanished from his eyes. Instead, they twinkled roguishly. "My pessimism has no place in your rosy young world. The universe should feel like your plaything."

Not really. It was the other way round. She was the universe's plaything.

"You shouldn't miss the last dance of the evening, Lady —" He stopped and shook his head in mock annoyance. "I haven't even asked an introduction or offered one."

As if she cared to know him. Or tell him who she was.

"CSA Stevan Helves," he informed anyway.

If she remembered correctly, CSA meant Chief Special Agent, quite a high rank at the GSO.

"May I know your ladyship's name?"

"Isbet," Ramya blurted.

His eyes narrowed, a bit too much and far too quickly. "Oh," he said. He bowed low. "May I have this dance?"

Why did he give her that look? Did he suspect she was lying?

"Lady Isbet?"

Just carry on, Rami! No one suspects anything!

"May I have this dance, m'lady?" CSA Stevan Helves asked again. An amused smile that rippled at the corner of his lips and crinkled his eyes suddenly made him look like a truant schoolboy.

Why not? She was going to dance with someone anyway, and he'd be easier to shake off than a fawning cadet before the dance officially ended. *Ten minutes — that's what I have to steal from the last dance.*

"Yes. Yes, you may."

They walked back to the banquet hall when the first notes were playing for the Decosset. Ramya spotted Isbet across the room, in Rownack's arms, laughing.

Good-bye, Isbet. Stay happy, my friend. Perhaps, someday, we shall meet again.

The music swelled and a whirling ocean of colors surged. Ramya glanced at the huge clock that hung over the gilded doors of the banquet hall. The long, jewel-studded hands had measured every second of the thirty-hour Confederacy clock precisely for centuries. Now it read 23:30. She would have to excuse herself exactly at 23:50. Until then . . . Ramya shut the world out and started her last dance, hoping to enjoy her final minutes at the CAWStrat.

5

The watch on Ramya's wrist flashed 24:05 in iridescent blue. Outside the balcony of her suite, the expansive gardens were quiet and dark except for the banquet hall and its vicinity. A breeze blew once in a while, cooling Ramya's sweaty forehead with a soft caress. The sky was inky; all three of Nikoor's moons — Alle, Rus, and the tiny Zieg — were yet to show up above the horizon.

Ramya slipped into a light jacket and adjusted her visor. With a quick glance at the mirror to check her plain street attire, Ramya riffled through her travel pack one last time. She had everything. She had tucked away her real identity cards far inside the travel pack and her visor was wide enough to shield her face and prevent security-cameras from identifying her. All she needed to do now was play the part of a commoner. If she could do that right, no one would ever figure out who she was.

"I can do this," Ramya whispered as she treaded lightly out of her room and peered into the long corridor outside. There was no one in sight.

She walked briskly toward the back staircase of the women's lodging unit the attendants used. Those staircases had to be monitored less than the main ones, she figured. The stairs were deserted, just like she had expected, and within a minute, she was outside.

Ramya moved closer to the shadows on reaching the grounds. On a moonless night like tonight, creeping out would be easy. She tapped the buttons on her watch to bring up a holo-map of the grounds. She activated the route to her destination, then broke into a run. She sprinted from the shadow of one tree to another, glancing back and forth for sentries each time she left the cover of the trees.

About halfway across the ground, Ramya stopped to take stock of the situation. It was 24:18. She had to get across to the gate closest to the banquet hall; that was where the shuttles waited for the hired help. The next shuttle—the one she had to catch before someone noticed she was gone—was at 24:30. The gate was five minutes away. Ramya checked the time again: 24:19. She adjusted the visor over her eyes and resumed her jog across the grounds.

She had not taken more than twenty steps when she heard the telltale beep of the sentry's comm unit. *God of the stars!* Ramya took a step back and then another, until she was well hidden behind a tree trunk. She could see his silhouette. Even in the dark his armor glinted menacingly. The sentry stopped a moment and looked around, then he started walking slowly in Ramya's direction.

Damn! Of all the directions he could go . . .

As noiselessly as she could, Ramya ducked behind some bushes. Twigs and leaves clawed at her; something moved under her feet. Holding her breath, Ramya waited. The sentry ambled along the pathway, but to Ramya's relief, he was soon gone. She checked the time: 24:24.

She pulled herself out of the bushes and brushed off some stubborn foliage clinging to her. Then Ramya broke into a swift walk along the shadows once more. Within fifty steps, she saw her destination—the shuttle gate. People—the hired help for the banquet—walked in a steady stream toward it. All she had to do was mingle in. Ramya's heart fluttered wildly with joy, and she had to struggle to compose herself.

It was 24:26 when she joined the line leading up to the clearance booth. Beyond the booth, about ten sentries stood observing the people who were leaving the CAWStrat. And beyond them, five shuttles were waiting, each for a different destination. Ramya had to take the one to the spaceport. Once there, she had to catch a ship off Nikoor.

Freedom! It was so near she could almost smell it.

"Miss," the booth attendant's sharp voice made Ramya's hands tremble. "Your pass please."

Keep your cool. Don't let your nerves show. Ramya pulled Isbet's fake pass out of her pocket while the attendant watched with a bored expression on his face. He flipped the card over a few times, and then passed it through the scanner. His brows knotted right away.

"I don't see you on the entry log for today," he said, eyeing Ramya suspiciously.

You're doing fine, Ramya reminded herself. "The pass I used to get in didn't have any credits left on it," she explained, keeping her voice as calm as she could. "This is an old pass. I've used it before—you could check your logs if you want."

The attendant looked at the pass and looked Ramya over once more. "Do you have any ID on you?"

Breathe! You'll think of a way out of this!

"I have a valid pass. Why do you need my ID? No one has asked for my ID before."

The attendant's brows knotted some more. "Do you have an ID or not?"

"Of course I do," Ramya said, throwing a quick look around. The line had grown long behind her—people frowning, shifting restlessly on their feet. She stole a glance at her watch: 24:29. Flashing an apologetic smile at the scowling attendant, she slipped an arm into her travel pack and pretended to fish for her wallet. "I'm sorry," she said, and raising her voice enough to attract the sentries' attention, "that damned wallet always hides when you need it. Give me a sec, I'll find it."

Just as Ramya had hoped, an armed sentry walked over within a few seconds.

"What's the holdup, Sett?" he asked. "Is her pass no good?"

"Umm . . . it's fine."

"There's a long line to clear," the sentry said in a snappy voice. "The shuttles leave in minute, so unless her pass is invalid you better —"

"Got it, got it," Sett replied hastily. He handed Ramya her pass and glowered at her. "Here, you're clear. Move on."

With a hasty nod at the attendant and the sentries, Ramya hurried out of the CAWStrat's gate. The shuttle to the spaceport was right up front and fairly empty. Ramya found a seat toward the back, pulled down the visor over her eyes some more, and waited for the vehicle to leave.

***

The shuttle's last stop was some distance away from the entrance of the spaceport. It dropped off Ramya and two other passengers on the side of a quiet roadway and drove away. The area was likely a souk — a market that was more of a trading post for space travelers passing through. The shops were somewhat empty so late at night, as were the streets. In a distance, a bright light shone like a halo over the buildings. That was the spaceport, Ramya deduced.

Ramya tapped her holo-map to life just to be sure. It was a fifteen-minute walk at most to the terminus where the spaceships gathered. Adjusting the straps of her travel pack, Ramya took off in a steady stride across the souk. A few people passed her by, none sparing her a second glance. Her mingling skills were surely good, Ramya thought happily.

Ramya stopped midway through her hike at a spot that was lit less spectacularly than where she had started from. Even fewer shops were open in this section, but one attracted Ramya's eye right away. It was just the thing she was looking for — an arms and ammunitions store. While Ramya always carried a baton that she could wield in her sleep, she didn't personally own a firearm. She had been trained to use them quite well at the CAWStrat. She simply hadn't needed one until now, but running off into the unknown with only a baton in hand seemed a little unwise. No one planned a trip to the outer colonies and beyond without having at least a quick and dirty mag-gun on them. She couldn't leave Nikoor without one. Ramya adjusted her visor, and with a quick look around, she walked into the store.

The Norgoran proprietor of the arms shop was as efficient as he was aloof, much to Ramya's relief. He only raised his purple brows once when he saw the 1000 Liere note Ramya brought out to pay before quickly shifting back to a stance of disinterest. He was obviously used to transacting with shady people, and that suited Ramya fine. She was done with her purchase within minutes. Her new state-of-the-art M-gun was secure in a holster that was partially hidden by her jacket. Ramya was sauntering out of the shop when the front doors fell open with an airy swoosh.

Two people walked in, a woman followed by a man. Ramya wouldn't have looked at them twice but for the oddness of the pair and the conversation she overheard.

The woman was tiny — short and slender — and reminded Ramya of a garden fairy who could be blown away by a summer breeze. Nothing else about her was frail though. She wore a dark shirt with rolled-up sleeves, her bare arms covered with intricate tattoos of thorny vines, skulls, and bones in shades of black and blue. She stomped through the door like a raging pit-bull on the loose, veins throbbing at her temples, fists clenched, and nostrils flaring. The regular-looking male companion with close-cropped hair and a stubby nose trailed behind her like a chastised pet.

"Iffin mess we're in now," the woman hissed at her companion on her way in. "What were you thinking, Flux? That man and that iffin cargo is our only way out of this shit, and you let him go?" She finished with a glare, and if glares could kill, this one would've toasted the man to crisp in a heartbeat.

"I was just trying to get a bite to eat," the man, Flux, said plaintively. "Haven't set foot on a prime planet in a year. Just wanted some hot grub. Didn't think he'd sneak away."

The woman lifted a finger to her head and drew some invisible circles in the air. "Didn't you get how loopy he is? If we can't find him, Flux, that'll be the last hot grub you ever lay your hands on. You hear me?"

"Calm down, Fenny," Flux said. "We'll find him. How far could he have gone in that condition anyway?"

The duo strode past Ramya, oblivious of her wide-eyed presence. No wonder the Norgoran didn't show any interest in her. Compared to characters as colorful as these, she was as interesting as a loaf of bread. With another look at the foul-mouthed, tattooed woman, Ramya walked out of the shop. Once outside, she rechecked her holo-map. The spaceport was right ahead. So close to freedom. Ramya's heart beat slightly faster, and she could've sworn the air was lighter and easier to breathe. She wanted to hop and skip the rest of her way but forced her feet to keep a steady, normal gait.

This spaceport, like most others in Confederacy space, had two docks: the passenger and the commercial. Space ferries, as well as ultramodern personal space jets, plied in the passenger section. The commercial half teemed with freighters big and small that carried anything from milk to ores to smuggled wildlife.

They'll check for me in the passenger jets first, Ramya reasoned. That a Kiroff heiress could venture into a freighter craft would come last to anyone's mind. She headed toward the commercial dock with resolute steps; her feet picked up pace at the thought of anyone coming to look for her.

They would start looking the moment she went missing at the banquet, and that, she deduced with a quick look at her watch, was twenty minutes ago. By now they could've stumbled on a motion capture of her slipping out of her room. She didn't have much time; she had to find a freighter to sneak into and get out of Nikoor or they'd find her and take her back to the CAWStrat and her father. That would be the end of her hope of being free, forever.

She was about three crossroads away from the entrance of the commercial docks when she heard muffled shouts coming from the alleyway she had just passed. Ramya stopped. Was someone in trouble? She turned to look and then hesitated. Perhaps just a drunken tramp having a nightmare.

She was about to head her own way when she heard a moan. Ramya weighed her options. Time was running out fast. Her window of opportunity was closing. She had to ignore the sound and keep going. But her feet stayed rooted. Another moan reached her ears. Ramya gritted her teeth as she pondered her options—none of them promising. *Just go,* she told herself. But . . . what good was she if she couldn't help a person in need? She couldn't just leave. She *had* to help.

Heart thrashing wildly against her ribs, Ramya managed five shaky steps to the mouth of the darkened alley. She could barely see, but she saw enough. Two men, their silhouettes large and imposing, were raining blows on a large mound heaped up against the wall. The mound didn't have to moan again for Ramya to understand that it was another man. Her sinking heart started to beat like drums at the pinnacle of a Decosset.

"This is none of my business," Ramya muttered. She knew it was more than likely a drunkards' brawl, yet her hand inched closer to the baton at her hips by instinct.

The more Ramya wanted to leave, the more her feet stayed stuck. Instead of running away like her brain told her to, Ramya did something else altogether—she analyzed the situation and evaluated her strategy. This was clearly not a situation for close-range combat. Even though she was more comfortable with her baton, the gun would be a better choice, Ramya deduced. Pulling the new M-gun out of its holster, she yelled in the loudest voice she could muster, "Stop, or I'll blow your heads off."

The duo spun around to look at her. The beaten man moaned and crumpled some more. There was a moment of silence before a cackle, harsh and boisterous, rang out.

"Hear that, Roden?" one of the men said, laughing. "A girl's gonna blow our heads off. Funniest thing I've heard in a while."

"Let's get her too," replied the other ruffian, emitting chuckles that reminded Ramya of a braying donkey. Then the man lurched toward her, and Ramya simply stood there, frozen. Then, just like a thunderstorm breaking suddenly, she snapped into focus and waved her M-gun at the man.

"Stop right there or I'll shoot," she said, trying to pull off the bluff of a lifetime. There was no way she could shoot. Her hand shook like a feather drifting in the wind, so she propped it up with the other. It didn't help the shaking any and the man kept on coming.

You can do it, Rami. You've shot plenty of targets at the CAWStrat.

But this was not just a target. It was a living, walking, talking person. A despicable one at that, one who was beating a helpless guy to death.

Come on, shoot, Rami!

The man was no more than five steps away when Ramya's trembling fingers managed to pull the trigger. All she felt was a shudder as the gun recoiled. Terror of being attacked by the ruffians, the bright flash of the M-gun, and a loud crash of a wall collapsing stunned her enough to feel nothing else. In the next second Ramya realized that she had missed her mark and both the assailants were still alive and standing.

Now they're going to kill me. Ramya's tense fingers curled around the M-gun as she waited for the men to charge. Instead, the two men fell back and tore off through the other end of the alley.

It took Ramya a few more seconds to walk over to the man the goons had been beating up. She turned the flashlight mode on her watch to look. The man—his clothes ripped and spattered with blood—had rolled up into a cocoon. A leather bag with a broken strap lay next to him. He groaned and mumbled in an incomprehensible stream.

Ramya pulled off her visor and ran her fingers through her hair. She had saved him from the ruffians. What now? What in the stars was she going to do with a wounded man?

"Hey," a voice shouted from the mouth of the alley. "Everything all right in there? Need help?"

Framed by the streetlight was the unmistakable silhouette of the tattooed woman and her companion from the arms shop. Perhaps they could take him off her hands.

"Yes," Ramya yelled back. "A man needs help."

They were next to her in a heartbeat.

"It's *him*," the woman said. "Is he dead?" She turned toward Ramya. "What happened here, kid?"

"I . . . I saw a couple of thugs beating him up. I tried to chase them away."

The woman and her companion, Flux, rolled over the beaten man and Ramya recoiled at the sight of the gash over his right eye. Blood poured from it, over his face and over the front of his shirt.

"Holy mother of stars!" Flux said under his breath.

"Is he dead?" the woman asked again. "Flux?"

"He's barely alive," Flux replied. "Got to take him to the medic right away though."

"All right, I'll call Wiz," the woman said. Pulling out a comm unit, she tapped a few buttons and yelled into it. "We located him, Wiz. He got beat up pretty bad. Can you get a transporter here fast?"

"Will do," a male voice crackled on the comm.

"And fast."

"Yes, yes, I heard you the first time, Fenny."

Ramya waited until the woman, Fenny, had turned her communicator off. "I should go," she said. She didn't have time. Her lease of freedom was running out, and fast. She had to find a freighter to get on quickly enough before every CAWStrat sentry was crawling over the spaceport. Besides, the Confederacy had strict laws about reporting crimes, and the current situation demanded a visit to the nearest constabulary. Ramya was not about to wait around long enough for that to happen.

"You live around here, kid?" Fenny asked simply.

"Um . . . not exactly around but—"

"What you doing out here so late at night? This isn't a good place to be."

Didn't she know that? The spaceport and its vicinity was a haven for muggers and robbers, just like the men who had cornered the poor man she had helped.

"I know," she said, reminding herself to keep her tone humble, to not come off so smug that Fenny would remember her. "I'm just trying to find a ride off planet."

"Ride? But this road leads to the freight ships. You need to take the next road. That'd take you to the passenger lines."

Ramya fidgeted. This conversation was eating up her time. "Don't have enough money to buy a passenger berth," she said hastily. "I was hoping to get on a freighter and work for board."

"Oh? Where you off to, kid?"

Impatience had let an unguarded moment creep in, and Ramya blurted, "Just away from this planet."

Fenny chuckled. "In a hurry to leave this iffin planet, huh?" she said. "Well, we are too. If the captain agrees, you might as well hop on board our freighter."

Ramya's ears perked up. They had a freighter? Obviously. The woman surely behaved like someone who had spent all her life on a freight ship. She should've guessed right away.

"What do you think?" Fenny asked.

Ramya didn't know what to think. She didn't know who these people were, and she didn't know what they were mixed up in. How could she decide? But then, her plan was to simply find any freighter to get off Nikoor. Was there a way she could tell if this crew was going to be worse than any other?

Fenny was staring curiously.

"Where are you going?" Ramya asked.

Fenny shrugged. "No idea. But off this iffin planet."

Ramya threw a quick look around. It was getting quieter and darker by the minute. She had to find a flight out quickly. She had to decide.

"Do you think your captain will let me in?"

Fenny chuckled. "I think he would. You saved one of his men after all."

6

The captain of the rust-bucket they called the *Endeavor* was seated at one end of the mess deck. His eyes were closed, just like they had been for as long as Ramya had been escorted inside the battlecruiser-turned-freighter. Whether he was sleeping or meditating, Ramya couldn't figure, but except for vigorously scratching the stubble at his chin every now and then, he barely moved.

Why in the name of the stars did she board this ship? Ramya cursed her stupidity over and again. She had fallen for Fenny's offer for a ride aboard the *Endeavor* like a silly moth offered a fire to jump into. She had followed Fenny, Flux, and Wiz when they carried the injured man back to their freighter. On reaching the *Endeavor* — which all three showed off as proudly just the way her father routinely showed off the newest additions to his personal space fleet to impress visitors — they escorted her to the mess deck and left her there.

Ramya looked around as she waited for the captain to finish whatever he was doing. The deck, lined with rows of tables and benches, was antiquated but clean. In a way, everything was . . . spick and span. Perhaps she was wrong to call the ship a rust bucket; perhaps they maintained it well enough. Although the *Endeavor* was ancient compared to her father's personal fleet . . .

"Yes?" a gruff, somewhat annoyed voice interrupted Ramya's thoughts. The captain had opened a pair of bleary green eyes and fixed them on her. "What brings you to my ship, little girl?"

Ramya flinched at his words. *Little girl? Really?* A retort came bubbling up her throat but she pushed it down. Now was no time to be sassy. She needed to get out of Nikoor quickly and this man could help.

"I helped one of your crew. Saved his life."

"So?"

"So . . . Fenny invited me up here. Said you're about to push off into space soon. Since I'm looking for a flight out, she said I could try asking you for a ride."

"What's your name again?"

"Rami."

The captain's left brow went up some. "Got a last name or that's it?"

There were a zillion last names Ramya could have told him—she had made a list of them since yesterday—but at that moment she felt annoyed like never before. The edges of her head burned with some invisible fire.

The hell with last names, the hell with fathers.

"That's all I have. Not good enough for you?"

The captain's brow came down, and an amused expression—if he was watching a pair of squirrels dance a Decosset—swamped his face. "It's good. Where are you off to?"

"The Fringe." Ramya watched his brows twitch again. Regardless, he seemed like the kind of man you were better off telling the truth to. She decided to be as candid as she could afford to be. "But right now, anywhere out of here would work."

"The Fringe?" the captain said, the corners of his mouth curling a little. "How old are you, girl?"

What did age have to do anything with going to the Fringe? Uncle Brynden always said, "All it takes is guts." She had plenty of guts. Besides, Ramya had often seen girls and boys as young as fourteen working on starships, and in comparison, at seventeen, she was ancient.

"Old enough," she replied.

The captain chuckled. "Your parents must have their hands full."

Frustration and impatience mixed together and formed an explosive mix in Ramya's head. Why did he have to bring up her parents? *Cool down, cool down,* she kept saying to herself. She couldn't afford to blow this chance; there was no time to go looking for another freighter now.

"My parents are dead," she said, looking away from the captain. She could feel his gaze on her face while she stared fixedly at a distant corner of the room. What he gathered from studying her, Ramya didn't know. She only hoped he'd pity her situation.

"All right," the captain said after a while. "But I can't give you a ride for free. Everyone on my ship works for food and board. You have to as well. Got any special skills?"

Ramya shook her head. At the CAWStrat they taught her plenty, but none of it was of any use on a space freighter.

"You can train me," she said hastily. "I'm a quick learner. I can do anything. I'm good with machines."

The captain busily scratched his chin and nodded. "Commander Pornell," he yelled at the empty corridor beyond the door of the mess deck. A man, possibly in his twenties, with scraggly shoulder-length hair and round eyeglasses, walked in right away.

"Yes, Captain?"

"Meet Rami, our newest crewmember. The medic will need all the help we can spare to get our champion back on his feet, so I've decided to hire Rami to be the medic's assistant. What do you think?"

"Good plan, Captain," he said with scarcely a look at Ramya.

The captain grunted and waved impatiently. "Take Rami to the medic, please?"

"Yes, Captain."

Ramya and the commander had nearly walked out of the mess deck when the captain called again.

"And Ross, ask Fenny to chart a course to Alameda. We are leaving in five."

Fenny was lounging on a bench right outside the mess deck, as was Wiz. It seemed to Ramya that they had all been lying in wait for the captain.

"Did you get in, kid?" Fenny said, sitting up hastily. She grinned happily when Ramya nodded. "What's the job?"

"Um . . . medic's assistant?" Ramya replied, trying to gauge from their expressions whether her new position was any good.

"Ah," Wiz said. "Medic sure needs all the help she can get."

That was no more than what the captain had said.

"Now that Flux and Fenny have gotten the man even more beat up," Wiz continued.

"That credit goes to Flux," Fenny said. She got off the bench and looked quizzically at Ross. "What's eating you?"

"We're going to Alameda. Leaving in five."

Fenny winced. "Not another iffin prime planet."

"Captain's orders, Fenny," Ross replied coldly.

As she walked to the nearest ladder, Fenny shot a look at Ross that was far from friendly. "Well, if we had remembered the captain's orders and kept our course, we'd not be in this trouble at all. But hey, no, we got to pick up survivors. We got to get tangled with the nasty Kiroffs."

The world around Ramya seemed to fade a little. *Kiroffs?* Did she hear it right? Fenny couldn't have meant House Kiroff.

"Don't forget I outrank you, Fenny," Ross yelled. "Besides, you're the one who picked up the distress beacon."

His words were lost on an empty ladder, as Fenny had disappeared long before he finished.

"This way, Rami," Ross said. "Let's go meet the medic before we take off."

"Good luck, kid," Wiz yelled. He too had hoisted himself up the same ladder Fenny used. "You must be excited."

Ramya forced a smile. *Excited? No.* Truth was, she was terrified. Not only had she run away from all she had known, but also she was headed to the Fringe—the northern outskirts of the Confederacy's domain—where very few people ventured. As if she weren't taking on enough hazard already, she had to have picked the *Endeavor* for her journey, a ship that was somehow entangled with the Kiroffs.

Ross waved. "Planning to come now or should I check on you tomorrow?"

Ramya's fists clenched at his terseness. For a second, she wondered if she should run away from the *Endeavor* and back to the CAWStrat. It still wasn't too late. But her feet followed Ross even though her brain wanted her to flee. With every step she took, the dread in her heart grew.

I can still go back and make up an excuse for Leona. Father will never know of this. And then . . .

"A strategic marriage is the best way you can serve House Kiroff," her father had written. "There is no reason to continue your education at CAWStrat. You will return to Somenvaar. While I arrange your match with a worthy line, you will prepare for your nuptials. Learning the etiquettes expected of a lady of a great house is no easy feat, certainly not for you."

Ramya's eyes stung thinking of her father's letter and a lump of pain grew bigger in her throat.

Be strong, Rami! Don't give up.

Ramya blinked, fast and furious. Gulping away the ache in her throat, she steadied herself. To her father and his house, she was only an object to barter and trade. His love she could never get, but even if she only wanted his respect, the only option was to fight for it. The only way to earn Trysten Kiroff's respect was to do what every Kiroff in the last hundred years had wanted to do but none succeeded — getting the Kiroff hearth back from the Moanus. That would silence her father forever. She knew it would be a long battle. This was just the first step, and she was thinking of giving up already?

Ramya strode faster to catch up with Ross. They walked along corridors that looked just like the mess hall — outdated, stripped of paint and polish, but clean. The ship had three levels at least, Ramya guessed from the sets of ladders going up and down at regular intervals. In-between there were a few elevators also. There were some layout diagrams posted at points where the corridors crossed, but the prints were faded enough to be illegible. The crew knew every nook and cranny by heart, Ramya deduced. She wondered how long it would take for her to remember her way around, and how many times she'd end up lost in the gray, maze-like corridors.

"Here," Ross announced. They had walked up to a large door that had been hastily and carelessly painted green. On it was a hand-drawn picture of an enchanted forest full of fairies, unicorns, blooming trees and shrubs, and everything else fantastic. Zigzagging across its top were letters in every color of the rainbow. Together they spelled "Medic's Magical Medical Bay."

"Wow," Ramya blurted.

Nothing was going be easy or as planned. But for now, the outdated *Endeavor* and its wacky crew would have to do.

7

Ramya sat on the old, lumpy cot in her newly assigned quarters and stared out the only window in the room, a tiny round opening with a rim spotted with tarnish. The chilly hardness of the bed made her painfully aware of the choice she had made — a life of a fugitive who had little else to bank on other than luck — and left her feeling as frigid and empty as the dark space outside the window. She had never been in a room so small, or so cold, or so threadbare. She had never traveled into space alone. She had never been so much in charge of herself and yet so helpless.

Ramya's fingers clutched at the worn edges of the mattress as she stared listlessly at the window in front of her. The panes were dusty, but that didn't stop Ramya from gazing at the planet they had just left behind. Nikoor shone like a green marble in space. Nikoor, the planet she had called home all her life, was receding fast. Very soon it would be out of sight and she'd be truly, hopelessly on her own.

But didn't she always crave for freedom? And for a chance to prove herself? *You did,* Ramya reminded herself sternly. This was her chance. There could be no room for fears. This had to be done. She had to chart her own destiny away from the Kiroff name, from Somenvaar, and from Nikoor. Perhaps her destiny was restoring the Kiroff legacy that had been stolen years ago. Only doing that could prove she was better than her father. There was no other choice but to show him she was worth something.

Ramya welcomed the swirling fumes of rage that came to life deep inside her. They grounded her, letting hope surge and drive the fears away. But helpful as anger was, she couldn't give in to it either. She had to keep her emotions guarded. There could be no room for error. Ramya closed her eyes and breathed in deep — the air smelled like metal and dust and was far from calming. Still she kept on breathing—in and out, in and out—until her thoughts had made peace. Then she walked over to the window and gazed upon Nikoor.

The biggest and the only significant landmass on it glowed like a jewel-encrusted tiara. Ramya's eyes picked up the position of Somenvaar in the southern reaches. *Does Father know I'm gone?* she wondered. She could see his clenched fists and tightened jaw on hearing from Leona how his daughter and heiress of House Kiroff had snuck out of the CAWStrat like a common thief. He would still keep his composure in front of Leona, but inside he would be fuming. What would he do after that?

"Rami," someone yelled from the corridor outside. Ramya recognized the voice of the petite, foul-mouthed woman, Fenny. She pushed her travel pack under the cot and yanked the door open. It parted with a loud groan followed by a long, annoying creak. Fenny didn't wait to be asked; she sauntered in and placed herself on the stool next to the window. "Thought I'd check on our special guest."

Her words were simple enough, but they made Ramya flinch. *Special?* Why did Fenny think she was special? Did she guess who Ramya was?

She brushed the thought away quickly. The Kiroffs were private to a fault, particularly when it came to the children. Ramya had been to public galas, but photos of her had yet to circulate the galaxy like her parents' had. Not too many would know what the Kiroff heiress actually looked like.

"I'm fine," she replied, trying to relax a bit. "So we're off to Alameda now?"

Fenny nodded, her light brown eyes scanning Ramya's face over and over.

"How long will the trip take?" Ramya asked.

"Five hours to the AP, and four more to the System V. Another hour or so depending on how quickly we get clearance."

Alameda was a prime planet, just like Nikoor. That meant it had strategic bases of the Confederacy on it. Nikoor was officially a prime planet being home to the CAWStrat, but cynics often said it was the Kiroffs' home that really mattered. Alameda, on the other hand, was home to the Kiroffs' staunchest rivals, the Arlingtons. However, the planet's prime classification was due to its being the seat of the GSO. Docking into Alameda, past all the security scans, wouldn't be quick.

"Anyway, we don't even know for sure if we'll go there in the end. If that iffin pilot could remember what had happened to him . . ."

She was surely talking about the man Ramya had saved, the one they had picked up from somewhere. *Where exactly did they find him?*

"Where are you from?" Fenny asked. "From this sector or out?"

"I'm from Nikoor. Not been outside the planet much." Ramya told her the truth. There was no point in lying about everything; she'd have plenty more to lie about anyway.

Fenny leaned forward with sudden interest. "You've lived all your life in Nikoor and suddenly you want to get to the Fringe? What happened? Someone died?"

"My mother," Ramya said quickly. She scrunched her face and looked away. She could feel Fenny's discomfort. "My uncle Bryn is the only family I have left. And he . . ."

Fenny's eyes turned into large brown headlamps. "Don't tell me he lives in the Fringe?"

"That was where he was headed when we last heard from him."

"But you understand that the Fringe is a *very* large place. And not a very welcoming place either."

Ramya shrugged, taking care to hold on to her doleful expression. It was indeed her plan to go looking for Uncle Brynden even though she had no idea where in the Fringe he might be.

"I'll find him," she said, watching Fenny's face soften. Ramya was not used to handling pity well, but she didn't mind it much now.

Fenny rose to her feet. "Well," she said, "I better get going. Don't you have to see the medic?"

The medic, of course.

"I will. The patient's sleeping, so the Magical Medic excused me."

Fenny gave out a throaty chuckle before walking out of the room. "Magical is right. A word of advice, kid," she said with a smirk, "stay away from her colorful concoctions." Then with a wink, Fenny was gone.

Ramya decided to spend a few more minutes in her room before heading to medical bay. She carefully pried open the cover of the climate-control module and stashed away her bagful of lieres inside it. After putting the cover back on, she checked the rest of her items. She decided to keep the baton with her but wrapped the M-gun with foil and hid it underneath the water dispenser.

She looked out of the window once more. In five hours they would reach the AP and board the SLH. She would be far from Nikoor. *Finally.* Happy as she was that she was out of her father's reach, Ramya also felt a pang, a sudden gut-wrenching emptiness.

"Don't be afraid, Rami," she muttered to herself, watching the green jewel-like Nikoor grow steadily smaller. "You'll be fine. You'll find a way."

Not wanting to let her nervousness take hold, Ramya headed to the med-bay. She remembered the path from her quarters to the med-bay, across two corridors and down a ladder to the colorful door. She took a moment to compose herself and then knocked.

The door fell open and a green smiling face peeked through it even before Ramya had rapped on it a second time.

"My dear Rami," said a voice that was no louder than a whisper, "you have returned."

"Yes, Domina Sosa. Thought you might need some help."

Sosa waved a slender six-digited hand. "Rami, Rami, Rami," she whispered as she shook her head. The steeple-shaped silken headdress atop her hairless head wobbled a little. "Address me as Sosa, just Sosa."

"Umm . . ." Ramya was not so sure about that. The green-skinned Norgoran medic was a royal presence. Everything about her — the

7

gentle voice, the flowing gait, and most of all the way she spoke—it all pointed to one thing: Sosa was of high-birth. Norgoran history was a major subject at the CAWStrat, but even before coming to the Institute, Ramya had been taught about their culture. As an heiress to a great house, she had to learn, not just about the Norgorans but also about all four races that made up the Confederacy. She had been taught to pick up cues and deduce social statuses of the other races at first glance and treat them appropriately.

Now after seeing Sosa's regal poise, Ramya could not make herself treat the medic as a commoner. Calling her "Domina" was appropriate, and even though she did not want to call her that when the rest of the crew was around, she could while they were alone.

Besides, even though Sosa's green skin was taut and glowing, and even though she was as nimble and deft as anyone else on the *Endeavor*, Ramya knew she was far older than any of the humans. Ramya guessed Sosa was near her fourth century, which was nearing the end of middle age in a Norgoran lifespan. Ramya imagined a random acquaintance calling her own sixty-five-year-old grandmother by her name and shuddered.

Nope! Domina Sosa it has to be.

"It's just a show of my respect, Domina," Ramya said, placing her palm on her heart, fingers outspread.

Sosa stared at her for a while, her mouth parting a little as if she wanted to say something more, but in the end she simply smiled and shook her head.

"All right, all right. Call me whatever you wish to call me. Sounds a little unfamiliar to these old ears, that is all."

With a final wave at Ramya, Sosa glided away toward a shelf stacked from top to bottom with beakers filled with colorful liquids. While Sosa mixed a variety of them in a long-necked pitcher, Ramya decided to look at their patient, the man she had rescued. He seemed to be sleeping peacefully in the bed farthest away from the entrance of the bay. Ramya frowned as she scanned the large vitals monitor hooked to the bed. In large glowing fonts, the machine presented a summary of the man's physical condition. It was the CHS, or the combined health score—a snapshot of the person's wellness—that worried Ramya.

Two hundred and fifty? That's too low! A healthy man of his age would be around a six hundred. He was hurt and sedated and far from healthy, but still . . . . Her frown deepened as she walked back to Sosa.

"What are you worried about, child?" Sosa asked.

Ramya buried an indignant snort with difficulty. From kid to little girl to child—what were they going to call her next? Baby?

"He's not doing too well, is he?" she said.

Sosa didn't seem perturbed in the least by her question. Perhaps she was used to seeing people with low CHS scores, or perhaps she knew how to mask her worry. Ramya couldn't decide which was true. The Norgoran woman had finished making a sparkling mix of red and blue liquid in the pitcher, which she now cautiously poured into two silver goblets. Once both of the goblets had been filled to the brim, Sosa pushed one goblet toward Ramya and picked up the other.

"Have a sip of my Pax Serengis, Rami. It will help you to put that anxious mind at ease," Sosa said between delicate sips.

Ramya eyed her goblet, remembering what Fenny had told her about Sosa's concoctions.

"Come on, child," Sosa goaded. "Take a sip."

There was no polite way to avoid this. She *had* to try it, Fenny's warning notwithstanding. Ramya brought the goblet to her lips, fascinated by the swirling reds and blues and the shining gold globules at the bottom. The Pax Serengis was warm on her tongue, and sweet with just a hint of bitter. Even before it had trickled down her throat Ramya felt her shoulders slacken.

Sosa's bright blue eyes danced. "It is good, isn't it?"

Indeed. The warmth inside her made Ramya think of the golden sands that bordered her home—the Kiroff castle Somenvaar—on the north, and the azure waters that rushed up to those sands. She remembered a summer, many years ago. Uncle Brynden had built a boat for her. He'd built it himself, a sturdy little thing made of planks and boards, without calling on the abundant help milling around the castle. A perfect boat it turned out to be, bright, shiny, and happy, unlike everything else about straggly-haired Brynden.

That was the last time Uncle Bryn had come to Somenvaar, and the last time Ramya felt someone cared about her. Uncle Bryn was very young then, maybe a little older than she was now, and even if he lacked in accomplishments, he didn't lack warmth.

"Always keep your chin up, li'l princess," he had said that day, ruffling her curls as he tugged the tiny boat out into the lagoon. "And don't let anyone tell you what you can be."

The sun had kept pouring over them in an endless shower of gold.

"It makes you happy." Sosa's soft voice broke Ramya's gossamer web of memories. "We need that around here. By the stars, those kids at the COM need to take a bottle of this every day, especially the captain. That'd keep their grumpiness away."

Ramya brought the goblet up to her lips again. She needed some badly, that was for sure. Sosa ambled off toward the patient's bed and a loose-stepped Ramya followed.

"We were not such a grumpy bunch usually, except for Milos and his pesky history with the Confederacy. But ever since we fished out this fellow" — Sosa lifted her goblet toward the sleeping man in the cot, his CHS now flashing two hundred and forty-four — "since we fished him out of that fleet debris, this place has been robbed of all smiles."

Ramya tried to focus her limp senses on Sosa's words. *What did Sosa just say? Fleet debris?* She thought she remembered something but it faded quickly.

Sosa went on. "Only survivor of such complete devastation. I have never seen ruins like it since the Locusta-Vanga war. He was doing just fine too, but then he had to run into those thugs. Now . . ."

"He will be all right, won't he?"

Sosa squinted at the man, her shoulders sagging with passing time. *She doesn't think he's going to get better.* The lightness on Ramya's heart brought on by Sosa's concoction lifted immediately at the thought of the man dying.

"Is he . . . is he going to die?" she asked.

Sosa shrugged and lifted her goblet again. "Only the stars will tell."

"But you're the medic. You must know."

"How much do I really know, child? Nothing."

Ramya pulled her jacket tighter around her. When had it gotten so chilly? She glanced at the man again, the CHS holding steady at two hundred and forty-four. If only she had come across that alley a few minutes earlier. If only she hadn't hesitated to intervene. Perhaps this man would have had a chance.

"Is it his head injury?"

"Mostly." Sosa walked to her table and picked up the pitcher of Pax Serengis. "Want some more?" She refilled her own goblet when Ramya declined.

"So that's why the crew has been upset. They should be, seeing him die after they got into the trouble of rescuing him," Ramya said.

"They're upset about a lot many things, but about him dying? Nah . . . not yet." Sosa walked away, sipping at her drink, to one of the windows of the med-bay. Nikoor was shining brightly like a green gem in the distance, much smaller than Ramya had last seen it from her own room. For a moment, Ramya was distracted by the beautiful view, but then she got back to Sosa.

"What do you mean, Domina? You haven't told them yet?"

"Do you think it's wise to pass the agony of failure to another before it's time?"

"But you know he's going to die."

The medic's eyes were glazed, as if she were gazing upon a

faraway vision. "I told you child, what I know is not enough."

"But the captain—"

"The captain needs him alive, but . . ." Sosa raised her left hand level with her eyes and turned it just as a child would twirl a colorful leaf, only there was no playfulness in her action. It was as if she were scrutinizing that hand, trying to find every flaw in it. "I failed him. I knew this man is important, child, but I couldn't—"

"You tried."

"Did I?" Sosa set her goblet down on the nearest shelf and trudged over to the window again.

Ramya's feet refused to move. What was wrong with this woman? From the manner Ross spoke to Sosa, Ramya had deduced her eccentrics were usual, but never had Ross come off as dismissive of the medic's capabilities. Yet now, the woman barely seemed in control. She was like this specter of a doctor, drifting through med-bay but robbed of physical ability to help.

The captain needed to know of the patient's condition. That much was not hard to understand. Sosa had lost her senses and the Pax was clearly at fault. Ramya had to do something. If Sosa was not willing to report the situation to the captain, then as her assistant Ramya had to.

"Domina Sosa," Ramya called. "I think we should inform the captain right away. And if you . . . if you don't want to tell him, then I can. Should I?"

Sosa turned around, a smile that seemed to be nearly as lifeless as the man in the bed behind them stretched across her purplish lips. She walked over to Ramya, and still smiling, picked up her unfinished drink.

"Medic," Ramya almost yelled. "You shouldn't be drinking any more of that."

Ramya thought Sosa's bright blue eyes flashed at her, or she could have been wrong. It was so short-lived that before Ramya could blink, Sosa's eyes had turned to their usual tranquil self. "I'm far too old for anyone telling me what I should be doing." Her voice reminded

Ramya of cold, hard metal. A sudden void came to life in the pit of her stomach. She had crossed a line. Ramya looked for a safe place to fix her gaze but found none. She wanted to turn away but her body was frozen. Only her heart pounded faster and faster and she stood there watching Sosa empty her goblet.

"You think I'm a fool, Rami?" Sosa asked in a glacial tone. "You know the captain and I have been friends for twenty years now. Why do you think that is? That's because we don't keep any secrets from each other, particularly not about patients in my care," Sosa informed, each word succinct and sharp. Thankfully her voice softened quickly. "Although, it's mighty noble of you to rise to the occasion to correct me. It takes courage to do that."

Ramya wished the floor would open up and swallow her alive. *Stupid, stupid, Rami!* How could she think the medic was incapable? She'd not been on the *Endeavor* for more than a couple hours and she had dared suspect the elderly Norgoran, her boss, of incompetence?

"I'm sorry," Ramya said, hoping Sosa would forgive her insolence.

"No matter," Sosa said with a casual wave. "You're young. You're nervous. You overreacted. It happens." She pointed at the now half-empty beaker of her concoction. "Some Pax?"

"No, no, I don't need any more of that."

Sosa clearly thought differently about the Pax. She refilled her goblet, and, closing her eyes, took slow sips at her drink. "You know why I'm so upset, child?" Sosa said with her eyes still closed. "I haven't had anyone die in my care in a long time. Besides, this man needed to live. He's the only one who knows what happened that day. He is the key to confirming our account."

Now that was new. Ramya leaned forward, the last traces of the Pax clearing from her senses. Sosa seemed to be sleeping, the goblet steady in her hand. As eager as Ramya was to know what Sosa meant, she didn't want to ask her anything. It'd startle her and disrupt her thoughts. *Besides, she'd wonder if I was too nosey.* Ramya simply held her breath and waited. To her relief, it didn't take Sosa too long to start again.

"It was a terrible day right from the start, and when we were thrown out of the SLH I knew right away that something bad was going to happen."

Ramya squinted at the Norgoran. Thrown out of the SLH? That was impossible!

"Sure enough, we came upon the debris."

"Debris?"

"Yes, a ruin like that I've not seen in ages. At least a hundred crafts . . . must've been an entire fleet. Destroyed. Blown to pieces. Poof!"

Suddenly, a memory of days ago zoomed out and hit Ramya. An entire GSO fleet had been destroyed in Sector 22, Isbet had said. It hadn't made any sense then, there was no ongoing war to trigger such devastation. Besides, as far as Ramya knew, Sector 22 had nothing worth having a whole GSO fleet stationed. It had been hard to believe the news Isbet had peddled.

Yet now, hearing Sosa's description of the massive wreckage, Ramya wondered. Could it be . . . ?

"Was this in Sector 22?" she blurted.

Sosa opened her eyes and turned. Ramya thought she saw a hint of disbelief in them, perhaps just plain surprise.

"Yes. But how do you know? Who told you?"

Ramya searched frantically for the right words. Being a student of the CAWStrat was how she had heard about it, and to be truly honest, had it not been for Isbet and her inquisitive ways, she too would have been in the dark. For a commoner that Ramya was pretending to be, it'd be unusual, if not impossible, to come across such information. The news about the destroyed fleet was being kept quiet, very quiet.

That was unusual in itself. Why didn't the Confederacy create the uproar that it was always intent on making? Were they hiding something?

Ramya realized Sosa was staring. If she couldn't tell her about being a student at the CAWStrat, then she had to go for the next best thing. "I worked at an eatery on Nikoor. The other day I was waiting on these two fine fellows from the CAWStrat. You know the institute down there near the spaceport? I heard them whispering about some top-secret stuff. You could say I got a little curious." Ramya flashed a bashful smile at Sosa and took a second to study the floor and trace a line on it with her toe. "They were talking about a GSO space fleet being destroyed at Sector 22. So, when you mentioned the debris I thought—"

"I see. Well, you're right. It was in Sector 22."

"Then he"—Ramya thumbed in the man's direction—"must be a GSO agent, right?"

Sosa shrugged. "We don't know. He was in a fighter craft when we found him. When the *Endeavor* reached him, he was not—"

A loud beep from the CHS tracker declared an emergency. Sosa rushed to the man's bedside with Ramya following right behind. While Sosa started fiddling with the setting of the support system hooked up to the man, Ramya's eyes were fixed in the CHS—it was falling rapidly. Two hundred thirty, it said one second, two hundred twenty-eight the next, and then the letters formed a jumble of red lights. It was getting awfully hard to breathe.

"Rami." Sosa said as she adjusted the drug dispenser, her fingers frantic over the dispensing controls. "I need you to find the captain. And I need you get him here as quickly and as quietly as you can. Do you understand?"

"Isn't there a comm?"

"You didn't hear me. I want you to get him quietly. Tell him it's time."

Obviously! Yelling for the captain on the comm would signal urgency. The rest of the crew could do without the panic. Ramya nodded.

"Go. And one more thing: you can take off for an hour or two.

Come back and see me after. All right?"

At least she wouldn't have to watch him die.

"All right." Ramya could hardly feel the floor under her, but she somehow managed to scramble. Once out of the med-bay, Ramya broke into an unsteady sprint across the corridor.

8

The COM was not too far away from the med-bay, only two levels up. The room's tight span was made tighter by the presence of four grown people. Captain Milos was scratching his chin thoughtfully at the center, his chair looking upon the other chairs in the room from a height. Milos and the three other people in the room—Wiz, Fenny, and Ross—turned to look at Ramya as soon as she stepped inside. Wiz smiled and waved, Fenny nodded, Milos let out a grunt, and Ross turned away hastily.

Ramya couldn't stop her mouth from twisting. What was wrong with Ross? Did he think acting dismissive was fashionable or something? Making a mental note to never smile at Ross again, Ramya walked closer to Milos. She didn't have to say one word. Milos rose from his chair and grabbed a jacket lying next to him.

"Sosa needs me," he announced, slipping an arm into the jacket. "Are we all set for entry into the SLH?"

"Yes, Captain. I can do it in my sleep. Except for . . . you know . . . those." Wiz punched a few buttons to make the visual on his screen larger and pointed at a distant cluster of tiny black dots on the screen.

"What in the stars are those?" Ross stepped closer to look.

Wiz shrugged. "Hard to see from here. We're still an hour out. But I'm guessing they are the SLH Troopers."

"Iffin ten of them," Fenny scoffed. "What the hell are they doing there?"

Milos headed toward the door. "They're not there to welcome us, I suppose," he said gruffly. "Commander, please secure our cargo. Take Fenny with you."

"Yes, sir."

"Wiz, can you handle the entry on you own?" Milos asked, his voice calm but tired. "I have to go visit Sosa."

"Sure thing, Captain," Wiz replied.

"Use the comm if you need me," Milos instructed before nodding at Ramya. "Let's go, little girl."

They walked out through the hatch, Ramya following the captain. As soon as they were a few steps away from the COM, Milos turned toward her. "Did Sosa have a message for me?"

"She said, 'It's time.'"

"All right. You're excused from med-bay for now."

Ramya nodded vigorously. Milos walked into the elevator right across from the COM. As the doors shut, Ramya thought how strange it was that both Sosa and the captain were so eager to excuse her from the med-bay.

This is a weird place, she thought. *They're mixed up in something that's for sure.* Was it something about the debris in Sector 22? Or the survivor they had picked up?

She had barely taken ten steps along the corridor when the doors of the elevator creaked open and Milos stepped out.

"Come with me," he said, marching back toward the COM and beckoning Rami to follow.

Ross and Fenny were hovering behind Wiz when they entered. They fell away like a pair of swatted flies on seeing the captain.

"I don't want to interrupt your ongoing investigation," Milos said drably. "Just came to remind you of our other cargo in case you've —"

"The iffin eggs," Fenny blurted. Her face wilted like fresh-cut salad under a summer sun.

"Yes, Fenny," the captain said. "Just in case, please go to the hold prepared."

"Damn eggs," Fenny grumbled.

"Yes, I agree," the captain said. He scratched his chin for a moment and then eyed Ramya. "Why don't you take her along? She'll learn a thing or two, and you'll have an extra pair of hands."

Neither Fenny nor Ross seemed to like the captain's suggestion.

8

Fenny gawped disbelievingly and Ross openly scowled before both protested.

"But she's just a kid, Captain," Fenny said.

"Sir, she'll only be a hindrance," Ross said. "She's untrained and . . . new."

While Ramya didn't quite understand what eggs they needed to secure and how she was going to help, the way Ross dismissed her yet again made her want to quash his head. *Hindrance? Really?* What kind of klutz did he think she was?

The captain's left brow had shot up. "You'll need the help. And she needs to learn the ropes."

"There's hardly time," Ross grumbled.

"Then I suggest you get started quickly, Commander," Captain Milos said before walking out of the COM.

***

Ramya followed Fenny and Ross to a room a level below the COM. It was the weapons storage room. The range of guns and munitions stacked on every shelf was an easy giveaway. But why in the stars did they need weapons to visit the cargo hold? Before Ramya could overcome the chill that had invaded the tips of her fingers and toes and was quickly streaming further up her body, Fenny handed Ramya some armor. It was a bulky brown thing of metal, as outdated a model as the ship they were in, but in pretty sturdy condition nonetheless.

Ross and Fenny donned their armor in silence. Ramya followed, hoping that no one would notice her trembling fingers. *Wish I had a glass of water. No, I need Sosa's Pax right now.*

"Here, take this," Ross held a medium-sized rifle and a flashlight out for her. "This is an Oori," he explained, pointing at the firearm. "It looks small but is quite potent. Use it only if you have to."

Ross picked a couple of large, mean-looking blasters and handed one to Fenny. Ramya noted the grim look on both of their faces. Why they were gearing up for battle, she still couldn't fathom. Since no one was explaining, she decided to ask.

"What exactly are we going to do?"

"Visit the cargo hold," Fenny replied.

"To do what?"

"Didn't you hear the captain?" Ross said. He was shoving handful of ammunition into the recesses of his armor.

"Of course, I did," she retorted. Why couldn't they answer a simple question? "I don't get why we have to dress up in battle gear to visit the cargo hold," Ramya said somewhat snappily.

"Because of the iffin eggs, that's why," Fenny replied. She busily checked her blaster settings and nodded at Ross. "Good to go."

"All right, let's move."

"Fenny, what about the eggs?" Ramya asked on the way down to the lowest level of the ship.

"They're not just any eggs, kid," Fenny said. "These are Pterostrich eggs."

Ramya had to clutch at her Oori tighter to stop it from slipping off her hands.

"Ptero-pterostrich eggs?" she stuttered to life after a while. "You don't mean those gigantic birds from Limitor, do you?"

Fenny nodded in a futile, hopeless sort of way.

"But they are dangerous predators," Ramya yelled, as if her calling them dangerous would make the current situation any better. "Why do you even have them in the cargo hold?"

"Long story, kid," Fenny said with a deep sigh. She stole a glance at Ross. "We would've delivered them to the Komilahns already had it not been for a detour. Now, we're stuck with them. And the eggs are about to hatch in our cargo hold."

Ramya gulped. It must've been noisy because Ross eyed her coldly. Ramya didn't care. She was going to face Pterostrich chicks in a few minutes, the commander's rudeness was nothing compared.

"So, we simply kill them, right?"

Fenny looked at her like she had just seen a ghost. "Hell no, kid. We kill no one unless they try to kill us first. All we do is make sure they're secure. That's all."

Ramya leaned back against the cold, hard wall of the elevator and closed her eyes. *God of the stars! What have I gotten myself into!*

9

The door of the cargo hold opened slowly. A chill drifted out from the dark insides as soon as the panels parted. But that was not what sent a shiver down Ramya's spine. It was the smell—a thick, suffocating smell typical of a wild animal's lair.

Let those chicks be dead already, Ramya prayed. *Please!*

Pterostriches were ferocious beasts. They were flightless birds with talons that were as big as a full-grown human's arm. Found only on Limitor, a tiny rocky planet in Sector 79, they were treasured for two things: their flesh was considered a delicacy and the young birds were used for racing. On Limitor, free of larger predators, Pterostriches had a thriving population. Yet, due to their ferocious nature, few were captured. The price of a live mature Pterostrich could easily reach a hundred-thousand lieres, so obviously there was no dearth of people trying to catch Pterostriches.

"Turning lights on now," Ross said, reaching for the controls on the inside wall. The ceiling flickered to life, bathing the space in cold, drab light, but only for a second. Then it was dark all over again. Ross tapped the controls a few times. The hold stayed lightless.

"Damn!" Fenny said. "Gotta get Flux take a look at that."

Ross slapped the bright red button of his wrist-mounted comm. "Flux, hear me?"

"Ross," Flux's voice crackled back. Ramya remembered the engineer; he was with Fenny on Nikoor. "Whassup?"

"The lights are out in the cargo hold. Can you fix it from your station?"

"Lemme check." He went quiet for a second or two. "I don't see any alarms up here, Ross. I'd have to check out the controls down there."

"All right. Do it later, but get to it today, all right?" Even before Ross switched the comm off, thoughts started pelting Ramya's mind. *What is wrong with this crew? They are wacky, grumpy obviously, but suicidal too?*

"What do you mean later?" she asked, incredulous. "Don't tell me we're gonna walk into that dark. There could be Pterostrich chicks roaming around in there. They'd be hungry. And—"

"And we're food. I know," Ross replied calmly. "But they shouldn't be roaming around. We put them in a cage."

Fenny snorted and Ross frowned at her. "In any case," Ross huffed, "we have to get inside and secure the *other* cargo. We can't wait for Flux to fix this. There's not enough time."

Fenny leaned closer to explain. "Ross is right. We have to get this done before we reach the AP. If the troopers board the ship and check the hold, we'll be in trouble. There's not enough time for Flux to come here and investigate. Besides, we can't let Flux in until we make sure it's safe in here."

Ramya shook her head. They couldn't let Flux in, but they could happily drag her along? Did they see a "Pterostrich food" label on her forehead or something?

"Those iffin troopers," Fenny grumbled. "What the hell have they lined up for? And not just one ship either. A whole iffin squadron. As if fugitives are on the loose or something."

Ramya's gut flipped. *Fugitives? What if . . . ?* She couldn't finish the thought. The wave of fear and nausea hit her back to back. Ramya breathed, slow and deep.

The panic subsided a second or two later and she forced herself to consider the idea. What if Fenny was right? The SLH Troopers could be checking for fugitives, for her. Her father could've easily gotten a squadron of troopers dispatched.

"Get your flashlights out," Ross commanded. "You," he nodded at Ramya, "stay between us. Fenny, I'll take the left."

His rough order, like a dog running through a flock of birds,

9

scattered Ramya's fears. Worrying was hardly of any help anyway. If the SLH Troopers were indeed after her, she was done for. Out here in space, she had nowhere to run.

"All right," Ramya replied eagerly, almost happy to immerse herself in the adventure. Fighting Pterostriches was better than coping with the idea that her father could be close — very close — to dragging her back to Somenvaar.

They filed inside. Ramya rushed along to keep up with Ross and Fenny. The door closed noisily behind them and the whole room plunged into darkness.

Ramya shined her flashlight around. The hold was huge, its other end hidden somewhere far in the darkness. The near vicinity of the room was filled with crates, boxes, and cages of all sizes. The walls seemed to curve and close in further ahead.

"There," Ross said, looking toward the left. Ramya peeked from behind him.

"Damn," Fenny cursed.

It took Ramya a second to fathom Fenny's frustration. Far to their left in the darkness sat a bunch of eggs in a thick wire enclosure. The spotted eggs were each about as tall as Ramya. There were four eggs and a giant heap of broken shells. Clearly, some of the eggs had hatched. Ramya tried to deduce how many — two at least! Whatever was inside those eggs was now nowhere to be seen.

"That's two iffin chicks missing, Ross. Where the hell are they?" Fenny whispered.

"Must be behind the other eggs," Ross replied. He didn't sound too confident of that assumption. "Come on, let's make sure."

Ramya didn't quite understand. What was there to check? A metal mesh — albeit not too sturdy-looking — surrounded the eggs. Even if a chick or two had hatched, they'd have to be confined within that cage. All was good, wasn't it? Was she missing something?

"Fenny," Ramya leaned forward to whisper, "they're in a cage. It's all good. Why are we even worrying?"

- 81 -

"Because this is a makeshift cage. Pterostriches are strong creatures capable of . . ." Ross let his words trail off, but Ramya could guess what he meant. They could break out of the cage.

"Why didn't you put them in a stronger cage then? You knew they were about to hatch."

Ross stopped and turned to throw an annoyed look at Ramya. "Because we haven't had the time. We've been running from here to there and having to rescue people who get into trouble, and responding to other people who won't shut up."

Jab complete, Ross resumed his cautious walk toward the Pterostrich cage. Ramya followed, fuming and frowning behind him. She had only asked a relevant question.

"Or perhaps you've been slacking," she said to Ross's back. He didn't turn around or stop, but did he slow just a tad? Good, that meant her retort had its intended effect.

"We just need to make sure they're all accounted for, kid," Fenny whispered. "Pterostriches can be wily."

Dimly illuminated by the flashlight, the gigantic eggs looked ominous. The emptiness that had been spreading at the pit of Ramya's gut now threatened to suck her from inside like a black hole. The tremble in her fingers had now spread to her teeth, and Ramya gritted them to keep them from chattering accidentally. She didn't need to give Ross another reason to mock her.

They found the newly hatched chicks, enormous red-beaked monstrosities, sitting behind the unhatched eggs. One of them raised a lethargic head on seeing them. Its eyes were dazed and as shimmery as honey in sunlight. There was something odd about that gaze, or perhaps it was some primeval instinct shining through that made Ramya fidget. She wanted to get away from the birds, as well as from their yet-to-be-born siblings.

"Let's set up a perimeter while we're here," Ross suggested hastily. "Then let's get out of here."

"Yes, that iffin bird is giving me the creeps," Fenny said.

Ramya agreed. They were creepy, especially the way its eyes kept lingering on Ramya.

"You stay here, kid," Fenny said. "Keep your eyes on the birds and your hand on the trigger. Don't worry. Ross and I will be back before you blink."

Both of them walked off to other parts of the hold, their flashlights sweeping the high shelves that lined the walls. Ramya waited, keeping her senses alert but avoided looking at the chicks' yellow eyes. She tried to forget where she was, but the chilly and stale air wouldn't let her.

Fenny and Ross returned soon with crates. Fenny pulled out two boxes of dog food from hers and together with Ross she deftly extracted their contents into an oblong plate. Then they placed the plate between the two adjacent bars of the cage and pushed it in.

"Must be hungry, poor things," Fenny said. Ramya could've sworn she detected a whiff of guilt in Fenny's voice.

Inside the cage, the chicks quickly moved their necks, their unblinking gaze studying the offering. In the next second, they were pecking away hastily at the meat.

"All right, now let's get started," Fenny said, beckoning Ramya over to where the crates they'd carried in. One of them contained three battery-powered spot lamps, which Fenny set up swiftly around the cage. The other one had a lot of loose parts, mostly long and black sticks and some wire. Ross pulled out a few and handed them to Fenny who promptly walked over to Ramya.

"These will make the post. Here, see, pass this one" — Fenny twirled the longer of the two sticks — "through this notch in the shorter one, plug it in this base, and there we have a post."

It didn't take them long to make sixteen posts. The chicks watched them work, their golden yellow eyes following the humans as they put up the posts around the cage and secured them to the floor with clamps.

"Rami and I can take care of the wires," Fenny said when the posts were set up. "You get the power."

Ross nodded and disappeared in the darkness. Ramya and Fenny had almost completed linking the posts with wire when he reappeared, dragging a large box behind him. Quickly, he pulled a pair of thick cables from the box. Ross plugged one end of it into a wall receptacle, and the other he connected with a clamp to the wire fence. Tiny red lights on the posts blinked in unison.

"There, it's up and running," Fenny said, observing the lights. "That electric fence should keep the chicks contained until we get the new cage ready."

"New cage?" Ramya blurted.

Ross's brows furrowed. "Weren't you the one accusing us slackers for not making them a stronger cage?"

He had her there. That had been her suggestion. But now, a different question popped into her mind. "How long do you plan to keep them here? You're not planning to raise them as pets, are you?"

Fenny shrugged. Ross looked disinterested.

"Perhaps before we go anywhere else we should deliver them to whoever had wanted them?" Ramya said, even though she knew her advice was unwanted.

"The Komilahns never buy hatched chicks," Ross informed with an air of derision, as if everyone in the galaxy was supposed to know that fact. He started gathering the tools scattered on the floor into one of the boxes.

Fenny explained, the way she always did. "The Komilahns train the Pterostriches for racing. They want eggs so the chicks bond with their owners right from the moment of hatching. It's too late for that now."

Ramya tried to gauge the unpromising situation. These people were unwilling to kill a chick unless it attacked, so simply spacing the eggs wouldn't sound attractive to them. They couldn't simply dump the eggs on the nearest planet and cause an ecological catastrophe. They could go back to Limitor and put them back where they belonged but surely there were other pressing matters the captain wanted to attend to in Alameda. Ramya came to the hapless conclusion: they were stuck with these hatchlings.

"Perhaps we could find another buyer," Ross said. He had gathered up the box and strode further inside, his flashlight carving a dimly lit path out of the darkness.

Fenny nudged Ramya's elbow. "Come on."

"Aren't you worried, Fenny?" Ramya fell in step behind her, shining her flashlight on both sides as she walked deeper into the unending stretches of the *Endeavor's* cargo hold.

"Sure am, kid. But we don't have much choice," Fenny replied. She sounded a tad exhausted, which was unusual for the woman. "The captain will think of something I'm sure. Right now, we have to make sure we're cool in case the troopers come in to check."

Ramya chuckled inwardly. Clearly, she wasn't the only one worried about the troopers. The *Endeavor's* crew was hiding something as well. Was it something they had picked up from the debris of the space fleet? Who was that man, the sole survivor of the Sector 22 catastrophe, who lay dying in the med-bay?

Ramya decided to probe a bit. "Cool? As in what way, Fenny?"

Fenny didn't respond. There was a chance she didn't hear because Ross was stomping quite loudly ahead of them, but it felt like she was ignoring the question on purpose.

What if they were carrying smuggled items? Carrying contraband was the way of life for the freight-ship owners. Most of them carried some smuggled goods—banned intoxicants, forbidden weaponry, you name it—among their cargo. The SLH Troopers didn't have to try too hard to find and confiscate prohibited items from the freight ships.

Ramya inched closer to Fenny. "We're not carrying contraband, are we?"

Fenny's head snapped around so fast, if someone had said the woman was a cyborg, Ramya would've gladly believed it. "We're not smugglers," she said, her eyes flashing. "Captain Terenze Milos would be the last one to break Freight Laws."

Ramya froze for a second. Fenny's sudden anger had startled her, but the name Terenze Milos gave her goosebumps. She'd heard that name before. Everyone at the CAWStrat—heck no, everyone in the Galactic Confederacy who knew anything about the Locusta-Vanga war—knew that name.

Ramya grabbed Fenny by the arm. "You don't mean . . . *the* Terenze Milos, as in the legend of the Locusta-Vanga war?"

Fenny shot an indignant look. "What? You didn't recognize him?"

No, she didn't. Who would've expected Terenze Milos running a freight ship as outdated and outmoded as the *Endeavor*, not to mention heading such a weird and wacky crew?

The Terenze Milos she knew was a hero of the War at Marsaan. His company had fought the Locustan fleet at Anomaly Point until only thirteen Wingers had been left standing. They didn't retreat; they held the Locustans until other Confederacy fleets arrived to help them. It was said that the galaxy would've been captured by the Locustans within a month if Terenze Milos had retreated that day.

Terenze Milos was a legend by the time the Locusta-Vanga war was over. Funny thing was, right after the Confederacy won, Terenze Milos had vanished. It was said that he was allergic to the heaping of praise and attention. Ramya had often wondered what had happened to him.

"Wow," she muttered. "I can't believe it."

"That's the captain for you," Fenny said. "And we're not smugglers."

"So . . . what is it that you're worried about?"

Fenny let out a gigantic loud sigh. Even Ross, who was about ten steps ahead of them, stopped and turned to look.

"Worried about our iffin luck. We happened to be somewhere we shouldn't have been, did something we shouldn't have done. And now they have us running from one iffin planet to another."

"Are you talking about being in Sector 22 when the fleet blew up?"

Fenny simply stared while Ross frowned down at Ramya. "How do you know this?" he demanded.

"Sosa told me. That's where you picked up that guy," Ramya said. She looked from Ross to Fenny and back. "I don't understand. You saved a man, did a good thing. What's the problem?"

Ross shook his head and resumed walking while Fenny shrugged. "We did plenty good, kid. Too much if you ask me. Don't worry. You'll see. The captain didn't send you here for no reason."

That was quite a riddle. What was she supposed to make of it?

A few steps ahead, Ross stopped. The beam of his flashlight was crisscrossing the dark space in front of him, and Ramya made out a faint silhouette. It was big, as wide as it was tall, and towered over them. Ramya strode faster, her flashlight aimed at the location Ross was pointing.

It was a nose, a gleaming silver nose. Ramya squinted harder. Could it be what she thought it was? She went one step closer. Yes, she had guessed right. It was a space fighter, a model she had not seen or heard of before. Even from what little was visible, the craft, easily three times the size of a single-seater Class 1, the size of fighters favored by the Confederacy, was in one word, stunning.

"That's the iffin goliath we need to keep hidden from the troopers."

"What is this? Where did you get it?"

"Same place," Fenny said with a shrug.

"Sector 22? But I thought all you found there was debris?"

Fenny and Ross exchanged looks. Obviously they didn't want to tell, but how long could they keep things from her? And what was the point? She was staring at their secret.

"I'm gonna piece it together anyway. It's not like I'm leaving anytime soon," she said. "Besides, like you said, when the captain sent me here, he possibly knew I'd see this and ask questions, right? Yet, he sent me anyway."

"Well, she's right," Fenny said.

Ross shrugged. "I'll set up the lamps," he said before walking away from Fenny and Ramya.

Fenny rolled her eyes. "Sure, leave it all to me. Ah, well. Here's the summary, kid. About two weeks back we found ourselves in Sector 22. There we came upon fleet debris. Don't know where it came from, or what caused the destruction, we just happened to be the first ship that came close. Would've steered clear of it, but picked up a beacon for help. So . . ." Fenny looked askance at Ross who had just finished setting up the three spot lamps in an arc and paid them no heed. "We went to help. Found that guy you saved on Nikoor. He was inside this."

Fenny raised her hands up at the space fighter just like she would be hailing the God of the stars.

"We hauled it in. Now we're on our way to hand this over to the Confederacy."

"I don't get it," Ramya said. "The Confederacy knows you have this. So why are you hiding it from the troopers?"

Fenny let out a long sigh and shrugged. "Because they . . . the Confederacy has asked us to keep it a secret. They don't want anyone to find out about it."

"But why wouldn't . . ."

Her words remained unspoken. Ross had flicked the first spot lamp on and it lighted up the entire craft.

"Wow," was all Ramya said.

The craft was unlike anything she had ever seen. It didn't resemble the GSO's standard Astro Scout, or the Wentworth-Busas favored by the Confederacy fleet. This space fighter was undocumented and unknown until now, at least for the general public. At first glance, it reminded Ramya of a predatory bird that was observing its prey from its roost.

"This is huge for a space fighter," she whispered breathlessly to Fenny.

Fenny nodded wisely. "Yes, it's bigger than anything the Confederacy has."

Its skin was made of an unknown dark metal—not polybdinum or infused-solandium like most space fighters of the day—and had a reddish gleam to it. It seemed to glisten and shimmer even in the bleak light. The nose was unexpectedly long and menacing for a craft of its type, if she understood the type right at all. A pair of massive appendage-like extensions in the front was now tucked under its midsection. Ramya couldn't see its hind from where she stood, but it seemed to have a couple of leg-like protrusions behind the craft as well. She couldn't tell whether these were landing gear or also housed weapons systems.

Ramya stepped nearer to inspect it closely. Behind her, Fenny and Ross discussed strategy for hiding the craft from the SLH Troopers. "A plasma-blending screen in front of it should do," Fenny said.

Ross shook his head. "The screens are too unreliable. We should sheath the body, use the Point Masks."

"But that'll take time. We'll need quite a few to cover all of it."

"Yes, but between the three of us we can get it done in thirty minutes, can't we? We just need ten of them on the top half, and —"

Their words faded abruptly. The world receded from Ramya, as if it had simply been a fake projection around her. All she saw was the logo imprinted on the underside of the craft. Ramya walked nearer as if she were in a trance, barely feeling the floor under her feet. There it was—the black circle and the three-taloned foot inside it. Ramya ran a finger over it. The mark stayed, dark and deep on the pale underbelly of the craft.

Let this be a dream, please.

Someone shook her by the arm, making her gasp. Fenny looked at her curiously. "Hey, you all right? You look like you've seen a ghost."

"I'm fine," Ramya replied, blinking rapidly. She was nowhere near fine. The black circle with talons inside it stared back at her. This was no nightmare she could wake up from, this was real. She looked up at the craft, her gaze trailing down its body and resting briefly at the logo before she forced herself to look away. This craft was trouble. They were *all* in trouble. If only she could tell them.

Ross walked over with a box full of silvery oblong things that reminded Ramya of detonator heads. He looked from Fenny to Ramya, his eyes narrowing a tad as they scanned Ramya's face. Perhaps he'd show some concern, Ramya thought. But she had thought too much too soon.

"Done with your sightseeing?" he said in his usual caustic way. "We've plenty to do."

10

Ross assigned Ramya the front section of the fighter to work on. The task was rather simple: she had to fix the detonator-type things — "Point Masks," Ross called them, apparently some sort of camouflaging device. If only she could keep her focus. She was distracted, and the sizable logo that stared at her while she worked hardly helped matters. Ross and Fenny had climbed up ladders to tackle the top. They worked mostly in silence, with an occasional banter or two, and Ross reminding them every now and then how much time they had left.

Ramya thought of joining the current conversation between Fenny and Ross about what could have caused the induction barriers of the SLH to fail when the *Endeavor* was spit out into Sector 22. But she couldn't hold on to their voices for two long, as her mind drifted off to something else.

A different time, in Somenvaar, eight summers ago. All she had wanted was to get her father to join her for dinner. Lady Sonya — the socialite lady of the house and her mother — was away on some visit and the grim darkness in the dining hall had kept morphing into weird shapes, wings and claws and pincers ready to attack. *Have to get Father to dine with me,* nine-year-old Ramya had thought. She hadn't found her father in his office that evening, but a large box next to his table had beckoned her.

Stop thinking about it, Rami!

Before Ramya could get lost in her memories, a shudder, like a twister ripping through her body, made her hands shake. The Point Mask slipped from her hand and fell on the floor with a loud clang.

"Everything all right down there?" Fenny yelled even before Ramya could retrieve the device.

"We don't have an unlimited supply of masks," Ross said. "Please don't destroy too many of them."

"It's fine. I didn't destroy it," Ramya shouted after checking the connection pins and the leveler eye. "I'm fine too," she added in an afterthought.

Her mind wanted to drift once more.

Stop!

Only, stopping wasn't easy. Ramya remembered seeing the logo on top of the box in her father's office, a black circle with fearsome black talons within it. She also remembered seeing a thick red liquid seeping out of the bottom. It wasn't a pool yet, but the base of the box was clearly soaked and barely able to hold its contents anymore.

Stop! Now!

She *had* to stop. Now was not the time. Perhaps, when she got a moment to herself, she could analyze the facts, but *not* now. Ramya yanked the fastener tight and moved to the next location. She started to hum, determined to keep the worries off her mind. She had to push out that bleakness from inside her. For now.

Ramya had five devices left to install when a comm beeped and crackled to life.

"Ross, hey, Ross?" Wiz said over the comm. His voice was tighter than usual.

"Wiz," Ross replied. "I'm here."

"You better hurry up," Wiz informed. "We're close to the AP, only ten minutes out, and the troopers are on the move."

"What do you mean 'on the move'?"

"Two of them are heading toward us."

"Damn! Is the captain with you?"

"Nope. He never came back. Still with Sosa, I guess."

"All right. Wait for them to hail you. Then keep a convo going. Don't let them board yet."

"Can't hold them forever." Wiz was starting to sound rather nervous.

"I know, Wiz," Ross replied. "Just do the best you can. We're almost done here."

"Hurry up. They'll dock in say . . . seven."

Right before the comm turned off, Ramya thought she heard a clang. She held her breath and tried to listen. Other than Ross and Fenny's breathing and the steady tinkling of tools, there was nothing.

"You heard the pilot, people," Ross shouted from above. "Let's get this finished.

Ramya picked up pace, fastening one Point Mask after another. She had gotten the hang of it now, aligning with two other Point Masks, fastening it to the body of the space fighter, and then turning it on to check if it worked. If the alignment was correct, the masks would emit a light, together forming an invisible mesh over the body of the fighter. So far, all of hers were working, and it was fun to see the bottom of the fighter disappear at the click of a button.

"I'm done," Ramya announced proudly after she had installed the last of her share. She had beaten both Ross and Fenny to it. Perhaps they had a few more to install, but she had to give herself credit, a moment to rejoice. After all, this was her first time.

Ross muttered something in reply, but Fenny shouted back, "Good job, kid."

Ramya was about to walk over to Fenny's side of the fighter when she heard it again — a clang, as if someone was hacking away at metal.

"What the hell was that?" Fenny said.

Ramya dove for her Oori. Placing a finger firmly on its trigger, she looked from side to side and into the darkness that blanketed the rest of the room.

"Probably just a rat," Ross said.

There was a faint tinkle, of something rapping on metal. Ramya gulped and fell back a step. Was it really a rat or . . .

Ramya looked up at Fenny. The woman was staring into the dark, her hand reaching for her own firearm that hung from the side of the ladder.

"Fenny, do you see anyth—"

The faint tinkle on the floor grew louder and faster before Ramya could finish her sentence. Ramya whirled around, but before she could lift her rifle, a chunk of darkness flew at her with a heart-stopping screech.

11

Ramya saw a flash of talons, feathers, and outspread wings before the ear-splitting screech made her legs buckle. The creature—a mass of gray and black and deadly bulk—leaped through the air toward her. It was a Pterostrich chick, its yellow eyes shining with hunger and a promise of death. Ramya heard yells, shouts, and curses. She lifted her Oori and pressed the trigger, doubting if her shots would land anywhere on the creature before it tore her to pieces. She scrambled backward, but the massive hulk plummeted into her with such a force that it threw her to the floor and pinned her down near the fighter's front wheel.

Pain erupted in Ramya's head, back, shoulders, all at the same instant. She screamed as the sharp talons dug into the parts of her body not covered by the armor, gouging flesh. The creature's red beak snapped inches from her face. Pushing the Oori as much as she could against the bird, Ramya pulled the trigger, over and over and over. The rifle shook, sending energy blasts into the creature, and slamming back into her ribs painfully.

The chick stared at her as if all those shots were merely a graze. Yellow eyes still focused on her face, it brought down its sharp beak with a mighty swoosh on her Oori wielding hand. Her rifle flew across the floor like a twig tossed into the air. Ramya heard her jacket rip, and under it her skin exploded with a sharp, burning pain. The bird seemed to teeter a little and Ramya didn't waste a second. Pulling her arms close to her body, she pushed them out in perfect synchrony, landing a sharp, double-fisted Molin slam into the bird's chest. The talons loosened, but not enough. Yellow eyes looked at her again, a pitiless red beak ready to kill.

I can't die. Not here, not now!

She had to break free. She writhed and struggled against those powerful legs that kept her pinned, all the while bracing for the pain when the bird would rip her skull open. The white-hot blast of fire that came swinging over her head was the last thing she expected. It singed her hair and landed smack dab on the Pterostrich's chest. The bird went careening, its talons still holding on to pieces of Ramya's jacket, its head thrown backward.

Ramya scrambled. She was shaking all over, she was covered in blood, and she didn't know where she was going. But she kept on going until a pair of arms wrapped around her.

"It's dead, it's dead," a reassuring voice said. "You all right, kid?"

Ramya breathed, long and deep. Each breath was painful, but they helped. Soon she was steady enough to answer Fenny's question.

"I'm all right," she said between gasps. "Probably torn in a few places though."

Fenny chuckled, the concern in her eyes fading a little. "Sosa can mend you easy," she said.

Ramya turned around to look at the monster bird. It was lying on its back with its feet up in the air. Ross stood next to it, studying it, his blaster aimed at its head.

"How did it get out, Ross?"

Ross turned a little, his sharp, appraising gaze sweeping over Ramya. "No idea, but we gotta check on the other one."

"Hope that's still in the cage," Ramya said. "I'm not in the mood for fighting another Pterostrich."

"Let's turn on the Point Masks and get out of here," Fenny said, and Ramya whole-heartedly agreed.

"You could take her to Sosa and I can clean up," Ross offered generously. In her mind Ramya balked a little. What had come over the commander? Was he tired of being snappy? Regardless, she didn't mind taking him up on the offer.

"I don't think so, Ross," Fenny refused. "Not after what happened just now. Rami's injuries are not that deep. Besides, we will be done in another minute or two anyway."

Ramya had to admit that she was a tad disappointed. She didn't want to linger in the hold another second. Thankfully, Ross was quick. In another minute he had turned all the Point Masks on, but the fighter refused to vanish behind a curtain of invisibility. Even though most of it was concealed now, the windows of the craft down to its nose were staring back at them.

"What the hell?" Fenny yelled, scowling at the fighter as if it was to blame for the failure.

"Alignment's off," Ross said. "We must've knocked something out of place when we scrambled down. Let me take another look."

Fenny grabbed his arm. "We don't have time, Ross. We have to get back to the COM. Wiz is alone in there."

"You go," Ross said. "I'll fix this."

"No," Fenny said firmly. "I'm not leaving you here. Besides, you're the commander. You need to be at the COM when the troopers board. We'll have to think of another way of hiding the craft from the troopers."

Ross shook his head and stared fixedly at the fighter's nose. "All this for nothing," he said a second or two later.

"Let's just go," Fenny said. "We'll think of something on the way out."

They trudged back, carrying the spot lamps along so they could have a clearer view of the room. Their walk back to the Pterostrich cage was slow, mostly due to Ramya's limp. Ramya didn't take up Fenny's offer to lean on her, but each step seemed to jostle every bone in her body. Everything hurt. Even breathing too fast or too deep made her chest sear. At least by the grace of the Gods, she hadn't broken a bone. The bird had not torn into her much either. Her jacket had taken the brunt of the assault, ripped and gouged and bloodied. She had to dump it, Ramya thought, sighing as a pang of sadness welled up inside her. The jacket was a gift from Isbet for her sixteenth birthday and the only thoughtful gift that year.

"It's still in there," Fenny said loudly.

They had arrived at the Pterostrich cage, and Ramya could see the other chick crouched in the corner. It briefly lifted its head up and looked fixedly at them before turning away with disinterest.

Ross shone a spot lamp at the top right corner of the cage. "There. That's where the other one got out."

"Makes sense. It got out through the roof and probably jumped over the electric fencing."

"Why is this one so quiet?" Ramya asked. She was half expecting the bird to charge at them.

"Who knows?" Ross replied. "Question is how do we patch up the top before those damn troopers walk in?"

That was another problem, probably even bigger than being found in possession of a strange space fighter. If a trooper walked in and got attacked by a Pterostrich chick, the captain of the ship would definitely be held liable for the injury or death. The Confederacy didn't take such offences lightly. The captain's freight license would definitely be revoked, and in the worst case he could be sentenced to a term in prison.

But there wasn't enough time to patch this.

"We could tell them there are chicks in here," Ross muttered thoughtfully.

"Some good that'll do," Fenny snapped. "You know how those iffin troopers are? They'll get even more suspicious and set a search party loose on us."

"No, they won't," Ramya chimed in. She had an idea that could work. "Not if they're scared enough."

Both Ross and Fenny turned to look at her. Fenny seemed curious, and even though Ross had gone back to using his cold stare.

"We could place the dead bird right there" — Ramya pointed at the door of the cargo hold" — and put some spot lamps around the cage. When the troopers come to check the hold, you could tell them about the attack. Obviously he'd refuse to believe you and ask you to open it up."

"That trooper will have the shock of his life," Fenny chortled, and slapped Ramya on the shoulder, which caused her to wince and groan. "I'm sorry, so sorry. I forgot," Fenny said hastily. "Are you all right?"

Ramya tried to dismiss Fenny's concern with a casual wave even though the stabbing pain in her shoulder had left her throat parched.

"This just might work. He'd probably refuse to get into the hold," Ross said.

"You think?" Fenny said. "Half of those gutless troopers wouldn't brave a full-sized rat."

Ross took care of moving the dead bird near the door. While he moved the body, Fenny placed the spot lamps in a ring around the cage and threw a canvas sheet over the broken section.

The set up complete, the trio had just walked out of the hold and into the elevator when Ross's comm beeped. Wiz's high-pitched voice erupted in a rapid stream of words from the device on Ross's arm.

"Ross, they hailed us. Asked to prepare a boarding ramp. I've just started the process."

"That's good," Ross replied. "How many of them are coming?"

"Party of four."

"All right."

There was a moment of silence before Wiz's voice screamed through the comm. "What do you mean 'all right'? They'll be here any minute and I'm alone in the COM. I've not heard a word from the captain, he won't even answer my calls. And you . . ."

"I'm on my way up, Wiz," Ross replied calmly. "I'll be there before the ramp is ready. Now calm down."

Ramya could hear Wiz inhale rapidly as if he were drowning.

"Long and slow, Wiz," Fenny said. "Long and slow. We're right outside the COM."

Ross turned off the communicator as soon as they walked out of the elevator. "Can you escort her to med-bay?" he asked Fenny.

Fenny grimaced. "You needed to ask that? Of course I will. Not leaving her alone."

"Fenny, I'm fine. I can get to med-bay myself," Ramya protested. Sure, she was hurting all over and bleeding in places, but she was well enough to walk down to the med-bay on her own. "Shouldn't you be at the COM when the troopers arrive?"

"I can handle the troopers," Ross replied. "I know you can get to med-bay on your own, but it's ship protocol that someone escorts you. I don't want to defy Captain Milos, do you?"

There could be no arguments after that. While Ross headed to the COM, Fenny led a limping Ramya away.

"Oh, by the whims of Dola!" Sosa invoked the Norgoran deity of creation—possibly her favored one—as soon as Ramya entered the med-bay. "What happened to you, child?"

"I'm fine," Ramya said, but no one seemed to hear her. Sosa sat her down on the nearest bed and started examining her while Fenny related the tale of the Pterostrich attack.

"Tell me you gave it a good fight," said a gruff voice behind her. Ramya had not noticed when the captain had arrived.

Ramya nodded, acutely self-conscious of her disheveled condition all of a sudden. This—scratched and torn by a stupid chick—wasn't how she wanted the legendary Terenze Milos to see her.

"I'm fine, Sosa," she protested again and tried to pull away from the medic, but the woman was having none of it.

"Rami, behave," Sosa said, arching her purple eyebrows ominously.

There was no getting past Sosa. And although Ramya wished the captain would leave, he didn't either. Arms crossed, he observed while Sosa checked Ramya, lifting one arm and then another, one leg and then the other, and so on.

Ramya flashed a smile at the captain, but there was an unmistakable glint of worry in the captain's eyes, something Ramya had not noticed before. He couldn't be too concerned about her; Sosa didn't seem very worried. Was he afraid of the troopers' visit then?

"Nothing broken," Sosa declared. "The wounds are not too deep thankfully."

"Good," said the captain. He turned toward Fenny. "I noticed a Trooper ship approach. Where are we with them?"

"They're boarding, Cap," Fenny said, and went on explain how the Point Masks had failed and their alternate plan with the bird carcass.

"Hmm," Captain Milos said. He scratched his chin and tugged his ears for a second or two, then nodded. "Let's head to the COM, Fenny. Let's greet the troopers." He tilted his head and gave Sosa a funny look. "Please have Ramya stay here. We need someone to be with *him*, and she could use some rest."

As soon as Captain Milos left the med-bay, Fenny in tow, Sosa flashed a bright smile at Ramya. "Let's get you inside," she said. "Follow me."

Sosa had a small medical bag in one hand and a pitcher of a familiar red-and-blue concoction in the other. She led Ramya to a side of the med-bay near the supply cabinets. Ramya craned her neck backward to check on the sick man and frowned. She couldn't see his entire bed from she stood, but the area seemed empty. Even the equipment that was scattered around his bed was nowhere to be seen. Ramya's heart sunk a little. The man's CHS had been falling when she had last seen him. That was why Sosa had sent her to summon the captain. What happened? Did he die?

Before she could ask. Sosa nudged her. "Sorry to rush you, child. I need to settle you down before the troopers visit. I do not like troopers in my med-bay. I always tell them, 'The med-bay is no place for strangers to barge in, it's a place of calm . . . peace.' Would they listen?"

Sosa threw a glance at Ramya that likely meant she wanted an answer of some sort, but Ramya had none to give. Her mind was whirring around the sick man and his whereabouts. Sosa went on despite her quiet, "No, they have no respect for the med-bay. They march in, stomping and thunking their boots like it is battleground."

"Domina Sosa," Ramya ventured the moment the medic quietened, "what happened —"

Sosa held up a hand. They had come to a tiny panel on the wall between two tall cabinets, each with elaborate paintings of vines and flowers on them. Sosa had placed her medicine box and the pitcher of Pax on a table and was hunched over the controller panel.

"Why do you always give me such a hard time?" Sosa wailed, fiddling with the control panel, fingers dancing impatiently on the glass façade. A bright red light on top blinked, as if with annoyance, likely because Sosa was not using the right code sequence to access whatever it was the panel was controlling. Ramya decided it was not the right time to ask the Norgoran questions. She leaned against a cabinet to brace her aching back and let Sosa continue her battle.

"Aha!" Sosa exclaimed after a while.

Ramya turned to look. The panel was now blinking green, and the cabinet to the right was slowly opening. *What in the stars!* The cabinet was no cabinet at all! It was a door, and behind it was another room, and in that room lay Sosa's missing patient.

"Come on in," Sosa said, walking into the cabinet with her bag and pitcher. As soon as Ramya stepped in, the door closed behind her. "You can stay here and rest while those star-forsaken troopers stomp through the med-bay."

Ramya was barely hearing anything. Perhaps she had been rattled by the Pterostrich attack; perhaps she was too tired, and now her senses were starting to grow blurry at the edges.

Sosa sat Ramya down on the other bed opposite to the one with the injured man and busily rummaged through her medicine bag. Ramya craned her neck to look at the man. He was in deep sleep. His CHS steady at three hundred now. That meant he was better. Still sick, but not dead.

"You moved him here? Why?" Ramya asked.

"Didn't I tell you about the troopers? They'll be all over the place disturbing peace. And that man needs peace and quiet. As do you. That's why."

That wasn't why, Ramya was sure. There had to be some other reason. Sosa was not telling the truth, and Ramya could tell from the Norgoran's quivering mouth and flitting gaze that she was not used to lying. She considered pressing her, then decided on a different line of questioning.

"Domina Sosa, you said you picked that man up from the fleet debris." Sosa nodded. She was bent over Ramya's wounds, cleaning and applying generous daubs of medicine on them. "Did he tell you what happened? I mean, who destroyed that fleet?"

Sosa stopped and sighed. Then she looked up, her eyes cloudy. "That's the problem. We know nothing."

"What do you mean?"

Sosa pulled out a large bottle with a sprayer attachment on top and lifted it up for Ramya to see. "This is going to sting," she warned, then misted Ramya's wounds.

Sting it did. Ramya could barely keep from yelping. Fists curled and teeth gritted, she somehow managed to handle the ordeal with just a few croaks and groans.

"Domina," Ramya asked when she had caught her breath. "The man . . . didn't he tell you what happened at Sector 22?"

Sosa finished packing her supplies, and after she had closed the lid of her medical bag, she poured Pax into two goblets. She pulled out a tiny container from her pocket, poured a drop or two of its contents into one of the goblets, and then held it out for Ramya.

"You're a persistent little bug, aren't you?" she said. "Drink!"

Ramya grinned sheepishly. She couldn't deny being curious.

"I just keep hearing bits and pieces that don't make any sense and —"

"I know. Besides, you're with us now. There's no reason to hide this from you. We have to tell you sooner or later."

That's correct. She would find out about whatever happened at Sector 22 sooner or later. Sipping her Pax, Ramya leaned back on the pillows and stretched her legs. The softness of the bed and the tingly warmth of the Pax in her throat were evilly comforting.

"We heard a beacon in the debris and found him. He was inside this gorgeous little space fighter that was glimmering like a gem. I'm no fan of fighter crafts, or any other craft, but I too was stunned by it. I'd never seen anything like that in my life." Ramya understood what Sosa meant. The fighter in the cargo hold was indeed breathtaking.

"We hailed the craft, but there was no response. So we pulled the whole craft in."

Whose decision was it to pull the whole craft in? Ramya wondered. That wasn't a prudent decision. The occupants of the craft were possibly unconscious, so pulling the whole craft in with tractor beams was a viable way to save the craft and the crew. But what if the craft had hostiles inside? It was clearly nothing like any of the space fighters anyone had seen. And the situation was quite eerie and strange—a lone fighter, unscathed in a sea of fleet debris. *Could an experienced veteran like Captain Milos make a choice like that? Or was it Ross?*

"We put it in the cargo hold and scanned for other survivors." Sosa took a long sip of her drink. "There were none. So, we headed for the nearest AP. While we were in the SLH, he made his appearance."

Ramya sat up. "Made his appearance?"

"Yes, almost like magic. His craft—the Striker—unfolded and he stumbled out."

"Striker?"

"Oh yes, that's what he called that space fighter he was in. Stryker, spelled with a *y* not *i*. It was one of the very few things he seemed to remember from before the incident."

"You mean from before his fleet was destroyed?"

Sosa nodded. "The poor man doesn't even remember his name."

"Really?"

"Really."

Isbet had said it was a GSO fleet, which justified the GSO recruiters that had descended on the CAWStrat.

"He works for the GSO, right?"

Sosa shook her head. "Why would you say that? I don't think he's GSO. He was wearing a black uniform with a strange logo emblazoned on the back. I've not seen that logo before. Nor has the captain. Or anyone else on this ship."

Why her heart started beating faster, Ramya didn't know. Then she realized why. She knew what that sigil looked like; she knew Sosa would soon describe a circle with outstretched talons inside.

"It was a circle with talons inside it," Sosa said, confirming her fears. "Three talons, or was it four?"

"Three," Ramya said.

Sosa took a swig at her drink and squinted at Ramya. "How do you know?"

"I saw it on the Stryker when we were trying to camouflage it."

"I see. Yes, three then. Anyhow, we don't know who he is."

"I thought you reported your discovery to the Confederacy?"

"Of course we did. That's when the trouble started."

Ramya didn't understand. Reporting the incident to the Confederacy was the right thing to do, so what was the trouble? Ramya tried to blink her tiredness away, but her lids were too heavy to move. It had to be the Pax. She could barely think anymore. All she wanted was a nice, deep sleep.

Sosa's voice was fading. The world around Ramya started to swirl at the edges like a giant wind spinner. When a heavy darkness poured over her senses and embraced her tired body, Ramya had no strength left to fight. She drifted unwillingly into a dreamless slumber.

12

It was awfully quiet when Ramya opened her eyes. For a second or two, she couldn't recall where she was. She simply lay staring at the metal rafters crisscrossing the ceiling. Then it came to her in a manic rush—her father's letter, Concert Night, sneaking out of the CAWStrat, the man attacked in the alley, taking off on the *Endeavor*, the Pterostrich attack. The memories left her shaking. Other details, such as the SLH Troopers boarding the *Endeavor* for a scan, trickled in.

She remembered the hidden room through the cabinet where Sosa had left her. Across from her was another bed where the man—the sole survivor of the mysterious space fleet wipeout in Sector 22—was sleeping. Ramya squinted to read the CHS monitor hooked to his bed. The numbers on it were a red blur.

She gave up trying to read the CHS and counted the rafters for a while. After she had done that three times over, Ramya decided to study her wounds. The largest and deepest gash was right below her left shoulder where the Pterostrich chick had sunk its talons. There were smaller tears on her arms and legs and a few scratches on her face. The wounds didn't bother her as much as the pain all over her body. Even moving a finger seemed to hurt.

If only Isbet could see me now, Ramya chuckled at the thought. Her friend would've wagged a wise finger at her.

"What were you thinking, Rami?" she would say. "How could you let your guard down around a Pterostrich? It's like meeting a boy with no makeup on."

"It wasn't a full-grown bird, Isbet. Just a chick."

Isbet would roll her eyes for effect. "It was still a Pterostrich, wasn't it? And what are you doing on *that* ship? Wait, is that even a ship? It looks to me like someone fit an engine to a tin can and chucked it into space. Get out of there, Rami. This doesn't befit you. Your father wouldn't approve."

Ramya banished the Isbet of her thoughts away. *By the God of the stars, Isbet, did you have to bring up my father?*

Tired of lying around and letting people lecture her in her thoughts, Ramya tried to sit up, but her back refused to help. "What did you feed me, Sosa?" Ramya muttered. The lack of strength was frustrating, and even though she could do little while inside the room where Sosa had her sequestered, Ramya craved for mobility like a beached fish yearning for water.

"Take some rest while you can. Stop being so impatient," Ramya chided herself, but that only helped for a minute or two.

"I'm not touching another drop of your Pax, Sosa," Ramya grumbled to herself as she struggled to push her uncooperative body out of bed. Lying helpless in bed, even in a hidden chamber, was unacceptable, especially when SLH Troopers were out and about. What if, by some weird stroke of luck, they found their way in here? She'd be a proverbial sitting duck. And what would happen if they were actually looking for her?

They couldn't be looking for her. Her father wasn't going to announce to the galaxy that the heiress of House Kiroff had run away. It would be shameful for him to admit that.

But even if the troopers weren't after her, they could recognize her. They would then surely tell Trysten Kiroff. And then?

They won't, Rami, very few people actually know your face. True, she was not one of those celebrities whose images were flashing on every billboard on Nikoor. Nor was she a most wanted fugitive.

Ramya was about to fade into a blackness when the sound of a groan drifted to her ears. It was not faint, but not loud either. It was perfectly timed. Ramya's senses alerted and focused on it, the weight from her limbs receded. Another groan and Ramya had found the strength to push herself off her bed. With slow, clunky steps, she crossed the distance—a seemingly endless ten paces—between the two beds.

The man was twitching, his face puckered. He was in pain, Ramya deduced. Her eyes scooted to the CHS monitor: four hundred and ten. His condition had improved, that was for sure. The man muttered something and shook his head a little.

Sosa needed to be here! Ramya stumbled back to the door and tugged the handle, but it didn't budge. Sosa had locked it from outside.

"Hey," a voice rang across the room, making Ramya freeze. She turned around slowly, wondering if she had heard right. The voice she heard was strong and could not be coming from a man who had been unconscious for a day. She wanted to rush to check on him, but she still wavered for a second or two. This, after all, was a man who had been the pilot of a ship marked with the dreaded black talons.

Ramya shuddered at the thought. Once again memories of that box in her father's office barged in. Ramya shook her head to drive away the nightmare she couldn't shake away even after ten years . . . the box . . . inside it a pair of severed human limbs. She still remembered the ear-splitting screams, a rush of running feet, tears . . . Her father had not held her close to console her. Instead, his anger toward her had multiplied.

"Never *ever* get into my office again, do you understand?" he had hissed while she sobbed in a cold, dark corner. "And not a word of this to anyone."

She hadn't dared tell anyone. The secret had stayed between her and her nightmares.

"Please, come here," the voice, insistent, dragged her into the present.

Leave him alone, Rami, every fiber in her being screamed. Yet Ramya didn't turn away. He was just a sick man. What harm could he do anyway? Besides, she'd just listen to what he wanted to say. She was the medic's assistant after all, and that was part of her duties. Ramya tiptoed back to his bedside and froze again.

The man was staring at her. It wasn't a vacant look, but boring into her with the sharpness of a well maintained drill.

"We're still on the *Endeavor*, I'm guessing?" The man paused to glance around. "Although this room doesn't seem familiar."

Ramya drew a long breath. A moment or two ago this man was comatose. How could he be so coherent?

"He sent you," the man said. "I was expecting him to be here, not his daughter."

"W-what?" Ramya barely managed a stutter. It was unbelievable enough that he was talking lucidly, but what was he talking about?

"I was expecting your father, Lord Paramount Kiroff, to come and get me."

A jumbled mess of words, thoughts, and fears streaked inside Ramya, leaving her gasping for breath.

He has recognized me. He knows I'm Trysten Kiroff's daughter. Ramya whirled around to check the door. It was still closed. Good. Now she had to convince him that she wasn't who he thought she was before Sosa came back in.

"What in the stars are you talking about?" Ramya replied casually, adding a chuckle here and there to make light of the situation. "Trysten Kiroff, you mean the head of House Kiroff, is my father? I think Sosa needs to up your medication some more."

The man's eyes narrowed. "I may be sick, but I'd recognize those eyes anywhere."

Ramya blinked. She did have her father's blue-gray eyes, but no one had told her the resemblance was that strong. Either way, she had to have him talking about something else until she found out a way to cover this up.

"I'm no Kiroff," she said firmly. Walking over to the panel that controlled the various medications Sosa had arranged for the man, she ran a hand over it. She wanted him to buy the part she was playing, of Sosa's assistant. "But never mind that. How are you feeling? I have to report to my boss, the medic."

The man smiled, a disbelieving, mocking smile. "The Kiroff heiress works for a Norgoran medic on a junk ship like this? That's something I won't forget in a hurry."

Ramya was not going to indulge him. She decided to steer the conversation away. "What's your name?" she asked, even though she knew he didn't remember it. Sosa had told her.

"My family name's Habardein," he said, smiling.

"They said you couldn't remember," Ramya said.

He chuckled. "I told them that. They were not letting me get out of this junk, so I got a little annoyed. But . . ."

The man's smile faded. He closed his eyes, brows coming together in a troubled knot. "I still can't remember my full name," he muttered, and took in a long, deep breath. "I just can't . . ."

Ramya leaned closer. "What exactly happened at Sector 22? Do you remember that?"

"There was a flash, a huge one. Something the other Strykers did. I don't know what. I remember hitting the beacon generator, and then nothing . . ."

"Other Strykers? They only found you and nothing else but debris."

"Yes, so they told me," the man said. He sounded tired. "But there were five Strykers in all. The rest of the fleet were regular GSO fighters."

So, there were GSO fighters in the destroyed fleet. That added up nicely. But why did the Stryker have that other logo on it? And what did her father have to do with any of this? This man should have been expecting a Confederacy officer, not Trysten Kiroff.

Ramya decided to probe some more. "The Stryker sure looks different from anything else in the fleet. Is it a new prototype of something?"

The man eyed her suspiciously. "You're a Kiroff. You don't know?"

Ramya leaned forward and looked him in the eye. "I'm *not* a

Kiroff. It's flattering that I look like golden-touch Kiroff, but I'm just a . . . nobody. Sorry."

That was not far from truth. Fact was, she could be a Kiroff a hundred times over, but she would still not know any of this. Her father wouldn't tell her even if he had partnered with another house in designing the Stryker. He didn't consider her worthy of anything, let alone secrets of a new prototype. Now, if he could get Ramya married into the right house, he'd surely groom her husband. Hell, he'd groom a pedigreed dog. Anyone but a girl.

But then, Ramya didn't always wait for her father to tell her. She had been hacking her way into the Kiroff data network for a while now. Ramya knew the Kiroff holdings, especially every factory that manufactured spacecraft. There was nothing in the Kiroff database about Sector 22, and no hint of a craft as unusual as the Stryker. Yet, this man was implying a Kiroff involvement. Could it be true?

The CHS monitor beeped and called for Ramya's attention. Three hundred, it said. He was destabilizing again. *Sosa!* She was about to try the door again when the man cried out.

"Wait," he said between short, raspy gasps, "stop." He was breathing fast, an odd wheeze sounded every time he inhaled. "You have to get my Stryker to your father. Fast."

The monitor had fallen to two hundred and ninety. He was fading quickly, and Ramya didn't want to spend any more time debating her identity.

"Why?"

"Because he needs to figure out what happened in that factory of his in Sector 22."

Ramya drew a breath. *A Kiroff factory in Sector 22?* Now that was news. As far as she knew, they didn't have a factory there. Heck, the Kiroffs didn't even have planetary rights anywhere in Sector 22. Was the man lying? Or maybe his lucidity was just on the outside when in reality he was not in his senses at all.

The man wheezed and continued in a tired voice, "He needs to find out what happened to the other four Strykers."

"What's special about these Strykers?"

The man paused to catch his breath, possibly to ponder how dependable an audience she could be. "They have Locustan tech fused into them." He heaved laboriously. "We were out in space testing out some new modules. We were doing well, but something went wrong with the others. I think they attacked the GSO fleet."

Perhaps that's how an entire fleet got decimated. But . . . four Strykers? Only four of them blew up hundred GSO crafts to pieces? Was that really possible?

A shudder rushed up Ramya's spine as thoughts bombarded her head. Just how powerful were these Strykers?

The man heaved. "I think they —"

He stopped, his words swamped by a gurgle. Drops of blood trickled past his lips.

"Sosa," Ramya screamed. She wanted to run to the door and pound it until someone opened it, but she stopped when the man struggled to speak.

"I think," he said, "I think the other Strykers might've signaled the Locustans. If they hear the call, there'd be war again." He stopped and wheezed. "And . . . and this time they'll have help on the inside."

What did that mean? If the Locustans heard the call, would they somehow open Anomaly Point again? Anomaly Point, the gateway to the Locustan world, had closed at the end of the Locusta-Vanga war. It had stayed closed since, but the worry remained that it could open again someday. Not knowing why it had opened and how to stop it in case it did again, the Confederacy had since erected stationary defenses in the area and also positioned several Confederacy fleets around it. But seeing how effortlessly the four Strykers had decimated the GSO fleet, would it be foolish to think they could easily bring down Confederacy defenses at Anomaly Point?

"I never thought this would happen, that the Strykers would . . . m-morph . . ."

Ramya had never heard of such a curious thing—a Stryker, a space fighter, morphed? What was it, a living being? And what did it morph into?

"Morph into what? What do you mean?"

The man didn't seem to hear her question. A vacant look had spread across his eyes. He went on, eyes drooping as he wheezed out words. "There's a spindle in my bag . . . tell Trysten they went rogue and . . ."

More blood welled up in his mouth. Ramya didn't wait to hear any more. She ran to the door and pounded it with every bit of strength she could muster.

13

Ramya sat stiffly on a chair with a meshed-metal back in Captain Milos's chamber. His room was sizable, fairly massive compared to what Ramya had been assigned, but it wasn't opulent or luxurious. A long desk with papers strewn all over it was on one end of the room, and a metal-frame bed that looked worn and lumpy stood on the other. The space between the two was taken up by cabinets of various shapes, all of them full of paper books in every size and condition. There were few knickknacks; some of them were interesting, like a large model of the galaxy at the center of the seating area where Ramya had been asked to wait.

Terenze Milos sat on an upholstered couch with ornate flower-patterned upholstery that made Ramya think of art from a Terran civilization. He drank a hot mix of milk and ground noja beans. It wasn't made the way Ramya was used to seeing it made. When mixed the right way with frothy milk, a noja was supposed to be a pretty shade of crimson. The one the captain was drinking was blood red and runny, which meant it had to be bitter as hell and near undrinkable. The captain kept sipping at it with such nonchalance though it almost felt like he was enjoying the taste.

A door opened noisily behind her and someone rushed in. Ramya did not have to look to know it was Ross. That was whom the captain had been waiting for before he started questioning Ramya.

"How's he?" Ross asked about the sick man as soon as he had closed the door.

"He has slipped into a coma. Sosa's trying to stabilize him, but I'm not holding out hope."

"Damn those SLH Troopers. They barely even checked the main level. We prepped for nothing. If Sosa were there with him, she could've intervened early."

"I wonder why the Troopers even bothered visiting," the captain said. "Anyway, Ross, have a seat. Are we all set for Alameda?"

"Yes, we're set," Ross replied while busily pouring himself a cup of noja from the fat flask set on a teapoy next to the captain's couch. "I haven't sent a message to the Confederacy HQ yet."

Captain Milos waved distractedly. "No need for that. We can announce ourselves when we get closer." The captain fell silent and thoughtfully rubbed his chin. "Something's brewing, Ross, and it's . . . not good."

Ross nodded and walked to the wall behind the couch. He leaned on it and took a long sip at his drink before squinting at Ramya. It was annoying to be watched like that. A highborn like her was used being stared at, but not like this, at close quarters and as if she was a saboteur caught in the act. Thankfully, even though it felt like forever, Ross did not look at her for more than a blistering second or two.

"So, why are we here, Captain?" he said, tearing his suspicious gaze away from Ramya's face.

"Our refugee, Habardein, has said some curious things to her," Captain Milos said. Behind him, Ross scrunched his face and glanced suspiciously at Ramya again. The captain continued, "I wanted you to hear this."

"Habardein?" Ross asked. "Is that his name? He told you?"

The last part of his question was directed at Ramya, and Ramya thought she caught a whiff of indignation in the commander's voice.

"Yes, he did," she replied, keeping a firm grip on her own annoyance.

"How did that miracle happen?" Ross asked bluntly. He left the wall and took a few steps toward the seating area. He looked at the captain and shrugged. "We've questioned him so many times and he hasn't once said his name."

"Memory can be tricky sometimes, Ross," the captain said.

"It's just plain weird," Ross said. "I presume he shared more than just his name or we wouldn't be here. All he's been saying to us is, 'Take me to Trysten Kiroff.' What's so special about this girl that—"

"Easy, Commander," the captain interjected. "Rami's helping us here. It's commendable that an ensign had the presence of mind to get any information from that man, especially after barely surviving a Pterostrich attack. I don't think she needs *us* attacking her now."

Ensign? Ramya straightened hearing the word. Did the captain just call her an ensign? That was the lowest denomination possible, so why was she feeling so giddy on hearing the moniker?

Ross pursed his lips and fell back a step, a frown still deeply etched on his forehead. A trickle of joy bubbled in Ramya's heart and she fought to suppress a grin. It almost sounded like the captain was proud of her, almost . . .

"You didn't know Habardein from before, did you?" Captain Milos asked, fixing his sharp green gaze on Ramya's face.

"No, of course not, I don't know him," Ramya said with a vehement shake of her head. She hadn't planned on telling them a few things, among them that the man was so angry with the crew he had decided to withhold all information about Sector 22. But now, annoyed by the way the men—mostly Ross—questioned her, she decided to come clean. "He didn't tell you because he didn't like you. He said you wouldn't let him contact anyone or let him off the ship. Why wouldn't you? He probably has a family somewhere he wants to talk to."

Ross crossed his arms and glared. "What a thankless bastard. We saved him, hauled him out of that wreck, and now he—"

"We didn't intend to torture him, if that's what you think," Captain Milos said abruptly to Ramya, cutting Ross off. "Since we were thrown out of the SLH, some of our own communication systems aren't working so well. Our long-distance transponders are messed up, so the next best way was to dock and use a public transponder to contact the Confederacy. Nikoor was not on our flight path; we simply docked here because it was the nearest space port from Sector 22."

Ramya felt an awkward tug in her throat. It was surprising how candidly the captain spoke of everything that had happened, as if he owed her an explanation. He didn't have to, yet here he was explaining his actions to a girl he barely knew.

"I couldn't let him off the ship until we had reported our findings to the Confederacy. As soon as Admiral Kanaa heard of this incident, she wanted us to leave Nikoor quickly and get to Alameda. She said everything we found in Sector 22 had to be brought to the GSO HQ. No one could hear about this until the Confederate Space Command had a good look at what we had picked up."

Ramya's mind raced to connect the dots. Not too long ago, she had suspected the captain of smuggling. Thinking about that now made her insides twitch with guilt. In reality, the captain was following a direct command from Admiral Kanaa, the top officer of the Confederate Space Command. Ramya had heard a lot about Kanaa—the woman had a reputation of outstanding intellect and strict principles. However, the order of absolute secrecy she had imposed on Captain Milos troubled Ramya somehow.

"That's why we had to contain the pilot," Ross said before sighing noisily. "Only the crafty bastard gave us the slip and got lost in the alleyways. Where did he think he was going?"

"To Trysten Kiroff obviously." Ramya couldn't stop the sarcasm from crawling all over her voice and as could be expected, the commander's jaws hardened.

"Rami," the captain said, "tell us what this man, Habardein, said to you. Please don't leave out anything."

One thing she was definitely going to leave out: the part where he called her Trysten Kiroff's daughter. Habardein had since slipped into a deep coma, and if she wasn't going to bring the topic up, no one would ever know. Besides, it was irrelevant information anyway.

Ramya related the rest of the conversation she had had with the wounded man about the missing Strykers and his fear of the

Locustans. As she spoke, the captain's brows bunched, and by the time she had finished Ramya thought she saw his eyes flash a few times. Ross however had paled considerably.

"So, Trysten Kiroff was running a research and manufacturing base in Sector 22," Ross went over the information Ramya just shared. "They were building fighters using Locustan technology when something went wrong. Something or someone destroyed the research center and the entire GSO fleet. Habardein thinks the four other Strykers did it. But why?"

Ramya didn't know how to answer that question. The captain didn't stir either. He seemed to have drifted into deep thought and he now sat stroking his chin. Something seemed to have thrown him off, because for the first time since Ramya had boarded the *Endeavor*, he looked angry.

"What did he say about the spindle again?" Ross asked Ramya.

"Nothing really. He was fading by then."

"Must be related to the Stryker we have in the hold."

"That's what it sounded like to me."

"Captain," Ross said, suddenly excited, "should we check that out?"

"No," the captain said so vehemently that Ross fell back a little. The sharpness in his voice was hard to miss as was the grimness etched on his face. "Leave that craft alone."

"But—"

"It's an order."

A dim-faced Ross took a step away and then another.

"We need to hand it over to the Confederacy as quickly as we can. We'd be lucky if we can without incident," Captain Milos said.

Ramya wondered what worried the captain so much. Was it because of the Locustan technology used in the Strykers, or was it because the Stryker belonged to her father? She hesitated a second and then decided to ask him.

"Trysten Kiroff would come after us, won't he?"

The captain looked at her, his worried gaze quickly turning mirthful. "He could come after us, but only if he finds out we have his toy. He doesn't know that yet, does he?"

It was the way his eyes twinkled and the words he used that made Ramya's insides squirm. Why did he ask her if Trysten Kiroff knew of the Stryker? How could she know if he knew? Was the captain hinting at her relationship with the senior Kiroff, or was it simply her fear jumping into conclusions?

"I wouldn't think so," Ramya said, forcing herself to stay calm. "Unless he has a gazing ball or something."

"Right," the captain said. A faraway look had descended on his eyes. He rubbed his knees the way Ramya often saw her grandmother do after she had been sitting a while. Then he abruptly lurched forward and rose. "I'm not worried about Trysten Kiroff," he said in a low voice, "but I'm worried about what he's been doing with Locustan tech."

The captain strolled to a bookshelf and started fiddling with a pair of shiny leather-bound books. Ramya caught Ross looking fixedly at the captain. The commander chewed his lips as he observed the captain, and Ramya could easily guess why. The captain knew something, clearly something worrisome about Locustans, especially having fought them for years during the Locusta-Vanga war.

It had been a vicious war. Ramya was a child when the skirmishes began, and Ross had to be fairly young himself. Most of Ramya's knowledge of the war had been from history books and from the stories her grandmother told her of her grandfather. Grappa Abelei Kiroff had been a starship captain who could have easily avoided the Locusta-Vanga war on account of being too old. But even though he was seven years beyond the age limit to be automatically summoned to the battlefront, fifty-seven-old Abelei rushed to command a starship. His was one of the first fleets to reach the frontlines that stretched along the Fringe. His was also one of the first ones that were eviscerated by the Locustan waves.

Ramya recalled what her Gramaman often said of Abelei's final message to her: "It's an unending sea of tiny fighters, Otis. Their dark, shiny bodies ripple like a wave in space, a wave of death ready to obliterate anything that comes in their path. It's a swarm like nothing else the Confederacy has ever seen, and looking at it right now, I know I'm not going to survive it."

Ramya fought the shudder in her spine, willing it to not spread across her whole body like it always did when she thought of Grappa's last words. He must have been scared. He fought and must have died bravely, but those were words of someone who was staring certain death in the face. The Locustans were a terrible nightmare, and that they retreated when they did was a stroke of fortune and nothing else. Had the Anomaly Point not collapsed, cutting off access to the Mehulian Quadrant, the Locustans would have kept on coming.

"Do you know what made the Locustans so fearsome?" the captain asked, strolling back to his couch with a dilapidated book in his hands.

"Their numbers of course," Ramya replied, recalling her numerous history lessons. "That there were millions of them in every wave and they never seemed to die out."

The captain nodded. "Yes, that's part of it. They came in incredible numbers to begin with. On every front, we were facing millions of fighters. They were small but they outnumbered us one to one hundred. When a swarm attacked, our biggest battleships fell within minutes. The Locustans' power is in their collective strength. But that's not all."

"Their regenerative power was an issue also," Ramya said eagerly.

"More than just an issue. On their colonies, Locustans are said to breed in massive hives. They are said to be manufactured. They inject a piece of Locustan DNA into an organic shell and a new Locustan in hatched within days. There's little time wasted in incubation, and since the Locustans mature fairly rapidly, a Locustan fleet can be raised quite quickly."

But that was not all either, Ramya knew. Even outside their colonies and during war, the Locustans bred. They seized enemy soldiers, people in the Fringe settlements, and turned them into organic shells on-the-go. While the Locustan army advanced, behind them their worker drones injected Locustan DNA into every organic thing they could get their hands on. The Locustan army was virtually endless and indestructible.

"They made Locustans out of our people too," she said gloomily.

"But, Captain . . ." Ross spoke suddenly, if a little hesitantly. "Why are you worried about that ship in the hold? Even if it had Locustan tech, it doesn't mean it has a live Locustan in it."

Captain Milos shook his head and rose once again, busily leafing through the book in his hand. It was a volume wrapped in brown leather and the pages were yellowed and pockmarked. Ramya tried to peek at the name, but the faded letters on the cover escaped her.

"The Locustan ships were an integral part of their hive, Ross," he replied, his voice fading. It was as if his thoughts were drifting. "They were not simply made of dead metals and synthetics like ours; they were all biomechanical. We didn't understand them then, but they seemed to have minds of their own. After the war, a faction in the Confederacy wanted to research the technology. But —"

"But the Locustan ships were all destroyed, weren't they?" Ramya asked. Recorded history said that everything Locustan was annihilated, including every Confederacy settlement the Locustans touched. The Fringe was said to have been an inferno for years.

"Obviously not," Captain Milos said, clearly referring to the Stryker. "I'd told them. I told the Confederacy to destroy it all, but they weren't willing to give up the chance to research Locustan technology. I grew tired of fighting my own people."

Was that the reason the legendary Terenze Milos quit the Confederate Space Fleet?

The captain continued in a heavy monotone. "Now I see they

didn't listen. They played with it. And now –"

A loud beep almost made Ramya jump. It was the captain's comm, she realized quickly. The captain quickly turned on the comm.

"Captain," Fenny's sharp voice filled the room. "Someone's hailing us."

Captain Milos's brows furrowed. "Hailing us? Here in the SLH?"

It was indeed unexpected. The technology of the SLH had few disadvantages, the prime of them being a lack of outside communication while a ship was inside it. Apparently, someone had overcome that problem.

"Yes, sir. It's a Lord Wultoph Aristide looking for the captain of the ship."

Fenny's words sucked away Ramya's insides in a heartbeat, leaving an enormous black hole. Chill, like frost spreading from the tips of her fingers and toes, rushed fast and furious to envelop her heart in a never-ending freeze.

Ramya knew that name well. Too well perhaps. Wultoph was her father's right-hand man, a lesser lord with rights to half a planet. Why was he here? What did Wultoph want with the captain? Was he calling for the Stryker, or had her father found out that Ramya was on the *Endeavor*?

Fear clawed into Ramya's heart leaving her breathless and devoid of hope. Did it have to be this way? Of all the ships in this galaxy, this was the one she had to pick? She wondered what fate had in store for her. Dragged out of here by her father, shamed and broken forever . . .

No! That couldn't be.

Captain Milos turned off his comm and frowned.

"Isn't that Trysten Kiroff's flunkey?" Ross said. "What could he want?"

"The Stryker," the captain replied.

"How does *he* know we have the Stryker? We haven't told anyone but the Confederacy."

The captain pursed his lips and shook his head. He and Ross

headed to the door with the captain leading the way. As badly as Ramya wanted follow them out, her feet didn't budge. It was not until Captain Milos had walked out into the corridor that Ramya forced herself up on shaky legs. She was not a moment too early.

"You coming with us?" Ross asked.

The captain half-turned to reply. "No, she doesn't need to. You should go take some rest, Rami."

"I'll go check on Sosa then," Ramya muttered. Wobbling a little, Ramya followed Ross out of the captain's chamber.

14

As soon as she was out of the men's sight, Ramya bolted, careening through the dull gray corridors that did not seem any more comforting than the colorless thoughts swirling in her mind. She wrapped her arms around her torso to stave off the chill. It hadn't felt half as bad when she'd boarded the *Endeavor*, but now the ship seemed like a gigantic cold storage. On top of that, she was aching all over from the Pterostrich attack.

Ramya barged into the med-bay a minute or two later. Sosa was reclining in her chair in her nook of concoctions. The Norgoran looked at peace surrounded by bottles with colorful liquids. A large black box sat on the table in front of her. Next to it was a jug of blue-and-red Pax Serengis—Sosa's favorite drink, and at the moment, Ramya was mighty happy to see it again.

Sosa opened her eyes as Ramya entered and the corners of her mouth crinkled a little. She reached for a goblet from the shelf nearest to her and slid it across the table toward Ramya. Then she pushed the Pax toward her and gestured for Ramya to take a seat.

All without a word, which was strange but good. Ramya was in no mood to talk to anyone either. She grabbed the goblet and poured herself a generous serving of the Pax. She knew Sosa was squinting at her, but she didn't care. Ramya gulped down a big sip of the bittersweet liquid, and a flood of warmth immediately washed away the all-encompassing dread inside her. Tedious thoughts gave way to colors of hope.

Nothing was lost yet. She had to keep on hoping. She was going to escape her father. She had to.

Ramya eased into a chair and took another long sip. Across from her Sosa had closed her eyes again. What Sosa was doing? Meditating or simply taking a nap?

She half turned to take a look at the sick man at the far end of the med-bay, noting the outline of his form through the transparent decontamination tent that Sosa had erected around his bed. Other than the incessant blinking of the CHS and various other monitors hooked to the man, all was quiet.

Until the black box on Sosa's table crackled to life. Ramya jumped and spilled a few drops of Pax from her goblet on her sleeve, making a bright purple patch on the green fabric. *Damn! This was a brand new med-bay uniform Sosa gave me,* Ramya thought irritably as she wiped the stain with vigor.

"Easy, child," Sosa whispered from across the table. "It's just a garment. We have more."

That was easy for her to say. She was not the one running away from Lord Paramount Trysten Kiroff whose long shadow was turning out to be harder to outrun than Ramya had expected.

The black box crackled again and Fenny's voice drifted in. "That's the Aristide channel hailing us again, Captain. Should I accept?"

"Yes," the captain said gruffly.

The warm fuzziness that had drifted over Ramya's senses disappeared in a blink. She sat up straight like a spring uncoiled.

"Are you eavesdropping?" Ramya whispered, pointing at the black box, which she now realized was a sound transmitter that was hooked up to the *Endeavor's* COM. Ramya knew Sosa functioned in her own swashbuckling ways, so she didn't question the legality of the snooping arrangement.

"Shhh . . ." Sosa raised a slender green finger to her lips. "We need to hear this. This is that skunk Kiroff's handiwork. All of it. Everyone knows this Wultoph guy is Trysten Kiroff's lackey. Now let's see why he's calling Terenze. Will be an interesting conversation."

Indeed. Ramya reached for her goblet. She was going to need a lot of help to get through this. It wasn't going to be easy discussing that *skunk* again.

A couple of sips later, Ramya leaned back into her chair and closed her eyes just like Sosa. All of her senses were focused on sounds as her heart braced to hear Wultoph.

"Lord Wultoph Aristide," Captain Milos's greeting floated out of the transmitter. The communication channel was open and working, Ramya deduced. "What makes you seek us?"

"Captain Milos," said a voice that Ramya had heard many times before. Wultoph Aristide was always by her father's side, like a shadow, almost like an extension of him. The Wultoph Ramya remembered was always quiet, calm, and collected. At the moment though, Wultoph sounded a surprised. "*The* Terenze Milos? I . . . this is unexpected."

"Good to see you again, Wultoph." The captain sounded sharp, cold. "When I last met you, you were just a boy trying very hard to get into the Space Fleet. I recall they kept rejecting you and your father was most disappointed."

The box stayed quiet for a long time. In her mind's eye, Ramya could see Wultoph squirm at the captain's jab.

"Didn't expect you to be running a freight ship," Wultoph said at last, and Ramya didn't miss the telltale dip in his voice.

"Don't tell me you forgot to read the *Endeavor's* manifest, Lord Aristide," the captain said with a dry chuckle. "If not you, I wouldn't expect such carelessness from your superior. Or perhaps he's slipping?"

A moment of uneasy silence hovered before Lord Aristide spoke again, now in a voice that was more robust. "That's beside the point, Captain. I'm here to ask you to return what belongs to us."

"I have nothing of yours."

"We know you do. And you'd be wise to hand it back to us quickly. You don't want to get mixed up in this."

"I don't know what you're talking about, boy. Go tell your boss I don't have time to indulge in this useless chitchat," the captain said brusquely. "Close the channel, Fenny."

"I wouldn't do that if I were you, Captain Milos," said another man, his tone bristling. It was the one voice Ramya was dreading and it left a trail of deadness inside of her. He sounded as cold and distant as always, but there was also something else in there—anger and frustration. For some reason Ramya could not fathom, a wee bit of glee stirred inside her on hearing him upset.

"Lord Paramount Kiroff finally emerges from the shadows," the captain said between chuckles. "I didn't expect you to come off your pedestal to talk to a freight-ship captain. You must really be desperate."

There was a tight pause. Her father had to be getting really annoyed now. Not only had he lost his Strykers, but also the decrepit freight-ship captain was openly mocking the all-powerful Lord Paramount.

"When I saw your name on the manifest, I couldn't believe it. *The Terenze Milos* running a freight operation in a bucket of bolts? What a place, what a crew," her father said, his voice seeped with ridicule.

"What have I always told you, Lord Paramount Kiroff? Never underestimate people or the choices they make. It's simply not wise."

Two things hit Ramya at the same time and made her stir. The first was immense respect for her captain. Terenze Milos was the first person she had seen who, even while addressing her father as Lord Paramount, seemed to have no fear or awe for the man. It almost seemed like Captain Milos was talking to a petulant little boy, and seeing her nemesis undercut like that was pure bliss.

Along with that came the realization that Captain Milos had known her father when he was younger. It made sense that since the captain and Grappa both served in the Confederate Space Fleet, they might've known each other and their families. Why hadn't she thought of that? And if the captain had known Grappa's family then, he'd have seen her as well. Did he . . .

No, he couldn't have recognized her. That was eleven, maybe

twelve years ago. She was a child then, much different from what she looked like now, or so she hoped.

On the transmitter, her father scoffed. "My mistake, exulted captain of the freight ship *Endeavor*. I didn't mean to offend you or your crew. That can wait. We have business to attend to now."

"We do?" Captain Milos couldn't have sounded more casual. "What business would that be?"

"You have something that belongs to me," her father said. "I need it back."

For a moment that was as dark as deep space and just as cold, Ramya thought he was speaking of her. Then the transmitter crackled with the captain's laughter.

"Not again. I just told your minion that I don't remember taking anything of yours, Lord Paramount. Where did you get such an idea?"

"You have a space fighter on your ship. It's called a Stryker. It's mine."

A sharp, unexpected jab of disappointment left a fresh gash in Ramya's heart. Perhaps in some unguarded moment she had hoped again, even among her fears of getting caught, that her father would be looking for her. But no. Lord Paramount Trysten Kiroff was simply after his missing Stryker. His daughter — missing or not — made no difference.

Her father's voice streamed in from the transmitter, "You picked it up from Sector 22 along with its pilot. Now, I don't care much about the pilot, but I want that fighter back. If you care as much about your ship and that crew as you seem to, you shouldn't spend too long denying what I just said. I know it's in there. Just hand it over, Milos."

Before Captain Milos could answer, a loud thump shook the table and made Ramya look up. "The cheek of him," Sosa snapped. She was sitting upright, glaring furiously at the transmitter, her curled fists placed squarely on the table. "The arrogant . . . piece of filth. Calling him by his name. No respect."

Welcome to my world, Ramya thought. This was what she had lived with all her life. Trysten Kiroff owned the galaxy and he sure wasn't shy of flaunting it.

"I don't know what you know, Lord Paramount," the captain replied calmly. Terenze Milos was taking it in stride. Even his voice was like still water that not even a ripple of annoyance showed. "I don't know how you know about anything in my ship. I do know that I can't help you. You—"

"The troopers picked up a solid reading of the Stryker, Milos." Her father's voice was just as composed. "You have it. I'll get it back one way or another. I don't want to hurt you or anyone else. Unless you make me."

"That's nothing but a threat," Sosa hissed. "Now I know why those darned troopers were blocking us. The minions came in to get confirmation for their evil overlord." Sosa filled her goblet to the brim with Pax and drank it all up in one breath. She plunked the empty goblet on the table and heaved noisily. "Oh, how I hate that arrogant man."

The captain's voice drifted out of the transmitter. "If you're sure of that then you should take it up with the Confederacy," he said in a voice tighter and snippier than it had been seconds ago. "You may be a great and powerful man, but I don't take orders from you, Lord Paramount Kiroff."

"You acknowledge having my Stryker then?" Trysten Kiroff's voice was steely.

"I don't acknowledge anything," the captain replied. "I think we're done here. I have nothing more to discuss."

"You leave me no choice but to board your ship and take what belongs to me."

"What?" Sosa and Ramya exclaimed in unison.

No, no, no! This wasn't happening! Her father didn't just announce that he was going to board the *Endeavor*. Where was she going to hide? How? Everything she had done in the past couple of days was coming to naught.

The captain's voice crackled. "And how are you going to do that? We're in the SLH."

Did the captain sound a tad defensive? Ramya couldn't be sure.

"You're in the SLH and we're still talking to each other, aren't we?" her father sounded smugger than ever. "When I want something, I get it. And I never make a promise that I can't keep."

A lot of things happened at that precise moment and Ramya didn't clearly understand the sequence of it. There was a mighty jolt that rocked Ramya out of her chair along with the jug of Pax that went flying off the table and crashed on the floor in pieces. Every bone in Ramya's body that had already been aching from the Pterostrich attack now screamed in agony as she fell in a heap next to the broken jug.

Fenny's yell filled the room in the next second, "Captain, we're falling out of the SLH. And . . . we're out. What the iffin hell just happened? Hey, there's a ship behind us. And it's trying to . . . Whoa! Wait! They've aimed a tractor beam at us!"

A rumble came from somewhere in the lower decks of the ship and once again the *Endeavor* lurched forward violently. Once again Ramya winced, every bone in her body screaming in agony.

Her father's taunting voice rolled across the med-bay. "I told you, Milos. You picked the wrong person to mess with."

"You're attacking a freight ship in Confederacy space," the captain said. "This is an outright violation of the Transit laws. You could kill civilians. Have you gone mad?"

"Not at all, Milos. I'm not going to kill anyone, I'll just get on your ship and take what's mine," her father replied casually. "Besides, the GSO's attacking you. Not me. I'm far, far away from where you are."

"Cut the channel off, Fenny. And get the shields up," Captain Milos barked. There was a sharp click and then a moment of silence before the ship rocked again. "I'm not sure how, but they're going to get in through the cargo bay," the captain yelled. "Commander Ross! Lieutenant Fenny! Grab your weapons and get there. Now."

"But, Captain," Fenny protested, "we need more hands here at the COM."

"We don't have more hands, so we have to make do with what little we have," the captain said. "You two get moving. I think I know what he's planned. He's going to teleport GSO agents into the *Endeavor* and get the Stryker out the same way. We can't let that happen. We've promised the Confederacy that ship."

"Teleport?" Ross asked. "You really think—"

"Yes," the captain replied crisply. "Go now."

Ramya could understand why Ross sounded so incredulous. For all the technological progress the Confederacy had made over hundreds of years, teleportation was something that never worked. There had been a whole lot of experiments, and starting with minor incidents like losing the tip of a nose to losing people altogether, they all failed horribly. Experimentation would have still continued but for the public outcry and protests. In the end, the Confederacy wouldn't allow it.

Yet the captain seemed to think her father had invented some kind of teleportation device? Could it be true? Who knew? If Trysten Kiroff had been experimenting with dangerous Locustan technology, what was teleportation compared to that?

"So?" Sosa's voice barged into Ramya's thoughts. The woman was firmly seated on her chair and she fixed a pair of sharp eyes on Ramya.

"What?" Ramya asked.

"You're not going to just sit there, are you?"

That was exactly the plan. Ramya had decided to sit this one out, make sure she was farthest away from her father's view. Stay away from his minions as well. Let the GSO come and take the Stryker, as long as no one was harmed. It didn't seem like her father was about to hurt anyone as long he got his toy back. This just wasn't a fight she wanted to get into. If only . . . if only Sosa would stop staring so accusingly at her.

"Do you need me to tell you what to do, child?" Sosa said, her voice barely a whisper yet taut like a whip. "They're attacking *your* ship, *your* captain needs more hands on deck, and you're sitting there like a . . . rock."

"The captain didn't call for me," Ramya retorted. A loud thud reverberated through the chamber and the ship lurched forward one more time. The GSO ship was probably shooting at the *Endeavor* again.

Sosa left her chair and teetered across the med-bay while the ship kept on rocking. She cast a scathing gaze backward at Ramya. "He didn't call for you, but that doesn't mean you should sit out a fight. That's no way people on *this* ship behave. If I didn't have a sick man on my hands, I'd be fighting alongside the others."

Ramya couldn't totally ignore Sosa's words, so she scrambled to her feet.

"Good. You're on your feet now. Now go report to the captain," Sosa said as she made her way across the med-bay.

Ramya stumbled out the med-bay and studied the long gray corridor that stretched on her two sides. She stared longingly in the direction of her room, thinking she could very well run there. Sosa wouldn't know until it was all over. Weird, terrifying groans of metal being assaulted by metal filled the air. The ship swayed and Ramya held on to the smallest depressions on the wall she could find so she wouldn't be thrown off balance by the constant rocking of the ship. It didn't seem like a ship as old as the *Endeavor* was going to survive this attack.

They were going to die.

Ramya dug her fingers deeper into a notch on the wall as a vicious hit almost made the ship tip over to its side. How could her father do this to a freight ship? How could the GSO aid him in this despicable plan? Wasn't the GSO supposed to protect every citizen of the Confederacy? Clearly, not any more. Now they were simply Trysten Kiroff's stooges assaulting a bunch of civilians who had done nothing wrong.

A little ball of anger at the pit of her stomach grew bigger as Ramya thought of the situation. Sosa was right; she had to fight. She had to stand by the man who had taken her in when she was desperately seeking shelter. She had to fight for him, her captain. There was a risk that her father would see her, but she had a find a way to help the *Endeavor* and its crew. This was not just another ship anymore: it was *her* ship and she was going to defend it.

Gritting her teeth, Ramya took a step in the direction of the COM, and then broke into a determined sprint along the corridor.

15

The captain was in Fenny's seat when Ramya skidded into the COM, panting to catch her breath. Wiz flashed a quick look before turning back to his station, but the captain growled at her without even a glance.

"I did *not* need you here, girl," he said. "You should be resting. If Sosa doesn't want you, go back to your room."

Ramya took a deep breath. She was not about to go back anywhere. She was not going to rest while her father and his stooges ripped the *Endeavor* apart. But she also had to be careful about saying that to the captain's face. He was, after all, the legendary Terenze Milos and there was protocol to be followed with a man like him, even if the *Endeavor* was nothing more than a freighter.

"Shields are up, Captain," Wiz informed. "And engine power at seventy percent."

"Good," the captain replied. "Get the engines to max power. We can't give them a chance to teleport. The shield should make it difficult, but we also need to maintain the distance."

Ramya took another step into the COM, her eyes glued on the large screen in front of the captain that displayed the back of the *Endeavor*. The GSO ship was hurtling toward the *Endeavor* at a breakneck speed, Ramya could guess from the flares behind the thrusters, but the distance between the two ships stayed more or less constant. The *Endeavor*, rusty as it was, still packed some power in its old engines. Since the ship chasing them was no lightweight, it seemed more than likely that the captain had updated the *Endeavor's* modules.

The GSO ship was large but not hulking, and if Ramya was correct, it was a state-of-the-art Starfighter Cutlass. No wonder her father was satisfied with sending just one ship after the *Endeavor*. The Cutlass was the newest and meanest Class-C battleship produced by the Kiroff factories and equipped with every weapon in the Confederacy's database. Her father made a fortune from selling them to the Confederacy.

Ramya's scanned the streamlined body of the Cutlass behind them, her eyes coming to rest on the two massive turrets on either side of the GSO ship. Whatever weapons those turrets could shoot had to be powerful enough to cripple the *Endeavor* in one shot, but strangely enough, the turrets were tucked in, which meant they were not planning to fire. That was hopeful. It seemed as if her father was only planning to get the Stryker and leave the *Endeavor* in one piece. It made sense—he wouldn't want an incident involving a freight ship. But would he want to leave witnesses after he'd gotten the Stryker back?

"What are you still doing here?" Captain Milos demanded, looking askance at Ramya.

"I'm here to help, sir," Ramya said as she tried to keep a steady gaze on the captain. "I don't know much about the equipment here, but . . . perhaps I can do something? Please?"

"There's nothing else other than equipment here," the captain replied.

Ramya shifted on her feet. Why was the captain refusing to have her in the COM? Was he worried about her health, or was he displeased with something she had done? A wave of self-doubt washed over Ramya's thoughts, and for a second her insides crumpled like a loaf of bread taken out of the oven sooner than advised. Still, one flicker of obstinacy refused to die down. No, Ramya decided, she was not going to accept being no one. She had to earn herself a spot on the *Endeavor*.

"Please," she begged. "There *has* to be something I can do. Maybe I can go help Fenny and Ross? I . . . I just can't sit around while these people keep attacking us. I just can't."

"It's catching up on us, Captain," Wiz yelled. "Engine power at max."

He was right. On the rear-feed screen, the GSO ship was getting larger by every passing second. They must've switched on a turbo mode to be catching up so fast, Ramya thought.

"How far are we from the nearest AP, Wiz?" he asked.

"It's close, Captain," Wiz replied. "Ten minutes . . . or less."

"All right," the captain said. "Maintain course for the AP. Keep engines at full power."

"But they're going to catch up before we reach."

"Yes, I see that. Since we can't avoid that, we prepare for it," said the captain. He ran his fingers over the controls on Fenny's station before rising to his feet. He looked at Ramya and shook his head. "You're stubborn. I was trying to keep you out of this because . . ." he let his words trail off and his gaze drifted. "Take Fenny's station and put on the communicator. I need you to guide Fenny and Ross when the GSO agents get on board. Can you do that?"

Ramya nodded furiously. She was in Fenny's seat before the captain could blink, and even though the wisp of a question trembled in her brain about what the captain had just left unfinished, the rush of excitement buried it promptly.

"So, we'll let the GSO agents come aboard?" she asked while plugging the communicator into her ears.

"We're almost within their tractor beam's range now," Wiz said. "They'll grab us any moment. Should we ready our repulsor cannons, Captain?"

"Not yet, Wiz. Not yet. How much farther to the AP?" the captain asked.

"Nine minutes, Captain."

"Stay on course, Wiz. Rami, ask Ross and Fenny to take position near the Stryker."

Ramya relayed the captain's order to Ross and Fenny, and after a quick study of the controls she was able to adjust her screen. It was now split in half with two views—one of the *Endeavor's* rear end and the GSO's Cutlass, and the other of the cargo bay where Ross and Fenny were setting up shop in front of the Stryker. The plasma-blending screen they had fitted on the Stryker still partially worked and it was weird seeing a bit of the space fighter peek out like an apparition. Ross and Fenny worked quickly, checking their weapons and setting up a perimeter of sorts around the Stryker.

Ramya scanned the other sections of the cargo bay and took a long look at the Pterostrich cage. To her relief, the lone chick seemed to be fast asleep. Ramya turned her attention back to Ross and Fenny, thankful that the lights in the cargo bay were back and she was now able to monitor the cargo bay from the COM. The last time they had ventured into the area when the lights were out, she'd been attacked by that Pterostrich.

"We're set," Ross's voice boomed in her ear.

"They're set, Captain," she said.

"Good," the captain replied absent-mindedly. He tapped his chin and leaned forward in his chair.

Ramya focused on her screen, specifically on the feed from the rear viewers. The Cutlass had now become a hulking presence on it. It drew closer and closer and then it seemed to stop. A flash of blue light—unquestionably a tractor beam—shot out from under its chunky frame. There was a hum and a rumble in the rear of the ship, and Ramya felt the *Endeavor* slow down. The tractor beam had found its mark.

"They got us, Captain," Wiz put the obvious into words. "We're slowing down. What should we do?"

There were more flashes on Ramya's screen, a few more hums, and the *Endeavor* slowed even more.

"How many tractor beams, Wiz?" the captain asked.

"Three, Captain."

"Charge up the rear repulsors and take aim. But don't shoot. Keep the engines at full power. How far is the AP now?"

"Five minutes."

On the array of equipment in front of Ramya, a large rectangular button flashed red and beeped. It said, "Incoming." Before she could turn around toward the captain, Wiz pointed at the flashing button and blurted, "They're hailing us, Captain."

The captain grunted. "What does Trysten Kiroff want now?"

His question blasted a hole through Ramya and for a second, the COM faded into specks of gray. Could her father be at the other end of the channel? What if he recognized her? *It's too late now,* Ramya chided herself. She took a couple of bracing breaths and fought off the fear. Adjusting her visor low over her face so the person on the other end of the channel wouldn't clearly see her, Ramya waited for the captain's order. It seemed to take too long to come, so Ramya shot a quick look backward. Wiz was looking curiously at the captain also. The button requesting a communication channel flashed with urgency of a man wanting a glass of water after crossing a desert.

"Captain," Ramya ventured. "Should we?"

He looked at her, his eyes narrow and his visage grim. "I don't know. Should we?" he said.

It was a weird question at the oddest of times. Ramya glanced at Wiz who looked taken aback as well.

"I think we should, Captain," Ramya found her voice first. "Perhaps they've changed their plans. Who knows?"

The captain's eyes narrowed to slits at her answer and he grunted once more. "All right then," he said finally. "Patch it."

Ramya slapped the flashing button and instantly an image started taking shape in between Wiz and Fenny's station. Ramya tugged at her visor once more and held her breath. She was going to need all her strength to see her father's face again. Ramya didn't risk turning her head up to look directly. From the corner of her eye, she could see a man in dark clothes standing at the center of a ship's COM.

"Captain Milos," he said, "good to see you."

Ramya let go of the breath she was holding. That was not her father's voice. It sounded familiar, but it was someone else, thank goodness.

"Good to see you, Lieutenant. You're holding us captive and I was told you'll board my ship and seize some of my cargo. So what are you waiting for?"

"I wanted to speak to you before boarding," said the man from the GSO ship.

"Hasn't everything been said already? Your boss, Trysten Kiroff, threatened my crew if I didn't oblige him. He told me his people were coming on board no matter what. What else is left to speak about?"

Ramya, still not daring to turn wholly toward the screen, continued to look askance. The man in the dark blue uniform shifted uncomfortably on the screen.

"My apologies for the situation, Captain," the man said. "Yes, we shall come aboard your ship whether you agree or not, but I still wanted to extend some courtesy."

Ramya turned a bit more to look at the man but still couldn't see his face clearly. The way he spoke reminded her of someone, she was not sure whom.

Behind her, the captain chuckled wryly. "Courtesy? You're about to take my ship by force and you want to extend your courtesy? Courtesy would be leaving us alone. Back when I was one of the GSO, that word used to mean something. Back when I knew Tuck. Long before your time, Gael."

The man on the screen fidgeted once more. "Perhaps it's time you caught up with the present, Captain Milos," he said. His voice had steeled.

"I know," the captain replied with a laugh. "I have a lot of catching up to do. Never thought I'd see an Arlington running around doing a Kiroff's bidding. Times have surely changed."

An Arlington in her father's employ? That was strange. The captain was right—the Arlingtons and the Kiroffs had been bitter enemies over ten generations at least. Ever since the Kiroffs had landed in the inner colonies and started building an empire for themselves, the Arlingtons were their rivals in almost every deal the Kiroffs fought for. More than half the time, the Kiroffs won. Being ousted from lucrative business deals, by hearth-less outsiders like the Kiroffs no less, did not sit well with the Arlingtons. The enmity thrived over hundreds of years to this day. Yet, clearly, something had changed for this man, Gael of the Arlingtons, to be working for Trysten Kiroff.

Ramya turned some more to look at him and then turned away in shock as recognition dawned on her. He had sounded familiar for a reason. He was the man she had bumped into in the verandah at CAWStrat, the one she had danced the Decosset with.

Ramya cringed. She had danced with an Arlington? And why was Gael Arlington working for her father? For money? Or was it something else?

There was so much Ramya couldn't fathom. Back at the CAWStrat, why had Gael not told her his real name? Had he recognized her? When she'd lied about her own name, he must've known who she was. Ramya tugged at her visor. She couldn't let him see her now.

"You do your catching up, Captain," Gael thundered on the screen. "My agents will be boarding your ship right now. I hope you'll lower your shields and not make us tear it down."

"Wiz, lower the shields for the boarding please," the captain commanded.

"Done," said Wiz an instant later.

"Touran Team, go," Lieutenant Gael Arlington of the GSO yelled.

Ramya squinted at the screen that showed the *Endeavor's* cargo hold. "They're boarding now," she whispered through her comm to Ross and Fenny.

"Close the channel, Rami," Captain Milos ordered. "We're done talking."

Ramya's hand flew in to smack the button off. She sensed a keen gaze sweep over her; whether or not it was Gael's she couldn't tell.

"Wiz," the captain said urgently, "aim our torpedoes on their impulse engine. You know where it's located on a Cutlass, right?"

Wiz nodded so vigorously that Ramya worried his head would fall off. But she understood his anxiety. Wiz had always seemed a nervous sort, and now the tension in the COM was as thick as a chunk of lard in midwinter.

"Good. Keep aim. Be ready to fire on my command," the captain said. He turned toward Ramya. "Ramya, scan every section of the ship. They'll likely show up at the cargo bay, but I don't want to miss them if they pop up somewhere else. There's no room for mistakes."

Ramya still didn't get what the captain was planning, but now was not a time to question, so she concentrated on the feeds instead. She also did not know how to look for signs of teleportation, so she simply scanned the ship over and over. On her third scan, Ramya noticed something odd in the cargo bay. The weird spot was smack dab at the center of the bay, halfway between the entrance and the far end where the Stryker was stored, and Ramya was certain she saw the air shimmer. She blinked a few times and looked again. There it was — a distinct wave rippled through the empty space.

"Captain, I see something," she yelled, pointing at her screen. She had no idea how she could make the visual bigger, so she hoped the captain would be able to see the strange disturbance.

The captain stepped down from his raised podium and rushed to her side. Leaning, he squinted at her screen. "That's them."

As Ramya relayed the information to Ross and Fenny, the shimmer grew more visible.

"Wiz, their shield has to be down now to allow the teleport," the captain said. "It's now or never. Are the torpedoes ready?"

"Yes."

"Fire all of them. Now!"

An indistinct rumble rose in the belly of the *Endeavor*, and Ramya felt the ship shudder under her feet and all around her. On the screen, five fiery balls streaked across the space between the two ships and impinged in a mighty wave on the slender extension right below the sleek upper frame of the Cutlass.

"It's a hit," Wiz shouted.

"Reload and fire again."

Another fireball erupted on the screen within seconds.

The captain had slipped back into his chair. "Rami, what do you see in the cargo bay?" he yelled.

Ramya eyes had been glued on the shimmer. She had seen dim outlines of bodies—armor clad and weapon bearing—in the shimmer just before the captain had ordered to fire, but right after, the outlines dissolved. Even the shimmer was gone now. She related that to the captain in one breath.

Captain Milos's lips curled just a little. "Wiz, shields up and repulsors on. Now!"

Wiz's fingers flew over the array of buttons in front of him. "Done and done, Captain," Wiz shouted, and almost immediately the *Endeavor* lurched forward. And then it fell backward again. Ramya held her breath. This seemed like an impossible battle. They were trying to break free of the tractor beams, but the dated *Endeavor* seemed no match for the Cutlass.

"Full power, Wiz," the captain yelled.

"It is at full power, Captain," Wiz shrieked back.

The captain tapped his chin. The *Endeavor* lurched forward one more time but it still did not break free.

"Keep firing the torpedoes. Now that they've pulled their people back, they must've got their shield up also. But we'll still cause some damage. They'll have to reroute some power from the tractor beams to hold the shield if we damage them enough."

"Why aren't they firing at us already, Captain?" Ramya asked. All the Cutlass needed to cripple the *Endeavor* was a big blast from the turrets that were tucked under its flared midriff.

"I don't think they want to take the risk of destroying us

altogether. It'd be an incident and they might also lose their Stryker."

Another volley of shots flew from the *Endeavor* and hit the Cutlass, and this time Ramya felt a stronger forward motion.

"Engines at full power, Wiz," the captain said. "And another round of torpedoes."

The torpedoes fired and the almost immediately the *Endeavor* shot forward. They were free for the moment.

Fenny's voice boomed in Ramya's ear, "What's going on? We seem to be moving again. What happened to the iffin GSO?"

"They didn't board, Fenny," Ramya explained. "We started firing before they fully teleported and they retreated right away."

"Where are we going now?" Ross asked.

"To the AP."

"Aren't they following us?" Fenny said.

"No," Ramya replied. "They're not moving. We might've taken out their engines."

"We'll pack up then?" Ross asked, and as soon as the captain answered in the affirmative, the duo in the cargo hold started packing the weapons.

On the rear feed, the Cutlass grew smaller as the *Endeavor* raced away. The GSO ship did not seem to move at all. The torpedoes must've got them good, Ramya mused.

"Two mins to the AP," Wiz announced.

"Good. Discard our planned route to Alameda. Find a path that'll be hard to guess. Doesn't matter if it's longer," The captain said. Wiz nodded. "And don't update the Confederacy . . . yet. We'll let them know when we get there."

"But they can track us on the Locator System, can't they?" Ramya asked, unable to keep her curiosity in check any longer.

The SLH network had a powerful system of tracking ships within it. As far as Ramya knew, if the Confederacy or the GSO wished to find out where the *Endeavor* was, they'd be able to do it without much trouble. The Super Luminal Highway was highly watched.

Wiz shook his head. "The Locator System only works close to the colonized planetary systems, not out in the middle of nowhere. Besides, it'd take a long time to find one ship in the cloud. It'll be like what they say . . . finding a needle in a . . . a . . ."

"A haystack?" Ramya completed.

"Yes, that one." Wiz nodded and smiled. "Captain, I'm going the Smyrnah route then."

Ramya recognized the name Smyrnah as a sparsely populated star system. The captain gave the pilot a grave nod.

"Entering SLH," Wiz declared. The ship shuddered and then it was steady again. Wiz flashed a huge grin at the captain and Ramya. "Safe and sound, but for how long is the question."

"It'd take Trysten some time to send another ship after us. I don't think they were expecting the setback we handed them. But now we'll have to keep them guessing. Pop in and out of the SLH, Wiz, and stay away from the big settlements. We should stay out of their sight," the captain said.

Wiz was hunched over his station, his fingers dancing over the controls. "Yes, we should be able to do that. We'll still make it to Alameda in six hours max."

"Good." The captain leaned back into his chair and exhaled. "Good work, both of you."

"Good work, Rami," Wiz said between loud chuckles. "She was as cool as a frozen Maritane. Who'd have thought this was her first time at the COM?"

Ramya felt a flush creeping up her cheeks when the captain glanced at her appreciatively. It was indeed a moment to cherish. She had done well, and perhaps for the first time in her life, Ramya felt like she belonged.

The captain left his chair and stretched like a cat waking up from a nap. "Wiz, can you handle the COM on your own? I was planning to get myself a cup of noja."

"Sure thing, Captain," Wiz replied cheerily. "Besides, I won't be alone for long. Ross and Fenny will be back soon."

"All right, little girl," the captain called Ramya and nodded at the door. "You've served your time and quite well too. Now off you go."

Ramya slid out of Fenny's chair and after a quick fist bump with Wiz, followed the captain out of the COM.

16

"Interested in a cup of noja?" Captain Milos asked when they had only taken a few steps away from the COM. "I make it extra bitter."

Even though the thought of being rude to the captain crossed her mind, Ramya didn't take her chances. She had seen the noja the captain made and even thinking of it brought up a shudder. She couldn't give herself up to the torture of drinking a bright red cup of noja, no matter who asked.

"Um . . . no," she said softly but decidedly. "I'm not a noja kind of girl."

"I know," the captain said. "You're a Pax kind of girl, right?"

Ramya's steps slowed right away. How did he know? Was her gait unsteady? Or did she smell of Pax?

The captain seemed to sense her questions. "When you ran into the COM, your eyes had a bright shine that I know only comes from Sosa's Pax," he explained.

"I was quite in my senses," Ramya blurted. "Wasn't I?"

The captain laughed throatily. "You know, I had doubted if you were. But turned out, you were good."

They had reached the captain's quarters. The med-bay where Ramya was headed was further down the corridor. Ramya slowed as the captain opened the door to his chambers and stepped inside.

"What made you doubt me?" Ramya asked.

Captain Milos turned around and looked into her eyes. His was a calm gaze, yet glinting with the sharpness of steel. Quickly they softened into a twinkle.

"If not for some temporary Pax-induced insanity, why else would anyone want to face the very monster they're trying to escape?"

Everything faded around Ramya. All that remained was the

captain's green stare and the wild thudding of her own heart.

He knows! He's always known who I am!

As Ramya stood rooted at the captain's doorway barely thinking or feeling, the captain scratched his chin and squinted. "Sure you don't want the noja?" he asked.

She wanted a whole jug of Pax. Where was Sosa when she needed her? Fear churned Ramya's guts as she stared at the captain's receding back. What if he threw her out? No! He wouldn't do that. If he wanted to throw her out he'd have done it already. Yet, he didn't. But why not?

The captain had walked inside while Ramya lingered at the door. He poured himself a cup of noja from his flask and raised it toward Ramya. "You can stand there for hours, little girl, or you could come in and we could have a conversation. Your choice."

That was a lie. She didn't have a choice. Like it or not, she had to have this conversation. As Ramya stumbled in, Captain Milos eased into his preferred couch. "Close the door behind you," he instructed, leaning backward to rest his head.

"Please don't throw me out." For all her resolve to hold herself steady, those were the first words to escape Ramya's mouth after she'd closed the door.

The captain sat up as if he'd been struck and a frown brought his brows together. "Why would I throw you out? You've proven yourself to be a valuable member of my crew. You've risked your life *and* your freedom to help the rest of us. Throwing you out would be the last thing I do."

"Are you going to tell everyone about me?"

The ghost of a smile scrunched the captain's face as he closed his eyes and shook his head. "No, it's not my secret to tell. Unless your lie threatens the safety of my crew, you can hold on to it."

What if her being on the *Endeavor* caused even more trouble for the captain and his crew? What then?

"Sit," the captain gestured at a chair across from him. He poured

16

a bit of his red, runny noja into a cup and held it out for her. "Drink this, you'll feel better."

Ramya took the cup but hesitated to bring it up to her lips, and her action was not lost on the captain.

"I know how your family likes their noja. With a lot of milk and honey, topped with cream, right? Well, this is different, but then," he leaned forward to look Ramya in the eye, "you're different as well, aren't you?"

There was no arguing that. Ramya took a sip and winced. It was bitter as bitter could be, and the harsh taste trickled past her tongue and seemed percolate into her bones like an acid tearing its way through slush. Yet, it was strangely refreshing. It cleared her senses and grounded her in an instant, like a miracle.

"There, you like my noja." The captain chuckled and took a long sip from his own cup. "Now you're officially part of the crew."

Ramya let out an anguished laughter. "So, everyone has to taste your noja to be officially in?"

"My noja and Sosa's Pax. And seems like you can handle both quite well."

Ramya couldn't stop the giggle. The captain was a strange kind of funny. And sitting there and drinking the undrinkable noja with him was unexpectedly relaxing. To be honest, it was the first time in a long time that she felt so much at home.

"So . . ." Ramya hesitated to bring up the topic that needed to be brought up. "When did you know about me?"

"When do you think?"

"Right when we met maybe?"

The captain took a long sip of his noja and nodded slowly. "Yes. The moment I saw your eyes, I knew. You have Kiroff genes, my dear. Your grandfather, your father, and your uncles, they all have the exact same eyes."

There it was again, the same conversation about her eyes. Not too long ago, the pilot of the Stryker had said the same. She had ignored

- 148 -

him, but if the captain had the same opinion then it had to be true. Weird thing was, no one had ever told her about it until now.

"I had known your grandfather for a very long time, Rami," the captain said. "So the resemblance is striking to me. But it won't be to everyone, if you're worried about that."

She *was* worried. She could do her hair a different way or dress and carry herself differently, but how could she change her eyes?

"Besides, you take after Sonya. A lot."

Her mother? That was new also. She did inherit her mother's dusky complexion but no one had ever mentioned a strong resemblance to the breathtakingly beautiful Lady Sonya Kiroff.

"How do you know Gael?"

The captain's question was so abrupt and unexpected that for a second Ramya couldn't fathom what he was asking.

"Who?" she blurted.

"Gael Arlington, the GSO lieutenant you heard speaking."

"I . . . I met him at the CAWStrat, right before I left. I didn't know who he was then."

The captain sat up, his eyes narrowed. "Gael was at the CAWStrat? What was he doing there?"

"GSO agents have been at the CAWStrat for a few days now." Ramya went on to explain the theory about the GSO recruiting cadets after their fleet was wiped out at Sector 22.

The captain sighed and fell back into his chair again. Staring at the ceiling, he scratched his chin for a while. Then he looked up at Ramya again.

"So, Gael was at the CAWStrat when you decided to leave?"

"Yes," Ramya said, sighing. Gael was very much there. She had actually left him waiting in the middle of the Decosset when she excused herself and pretended to visit the refreshment room. In truth, she had ran back to her room and taken off from there.

The captain took another sip of his noja before looking intently at Ramya. "What's you plan? Where are you off to?"

Ramya stiffened. She wondered if she could tell him about her plans to confront the Moanus and get the Kiroff hearth back from them, or if she could tell him about finding Uncle Bryn. Both plans were far-fetched, she knew. And he'd surely laugh at her.

"That's all right of you don't want to tell me," the captain said. "Everyone has a right to their secrets." His eyes took on a faraway look, and Ramya wondered how many secrets the captain had stored away in his mind.

"It's not . . ." She wanted to tell him she didn't care much about keeping her plans secret but that she feared ridicule, but her words faltered yet again.

"There's no rush, little girl," the captain said reassuringly. "It's not like we're running off anywhere."

"I'm headed for the Fringe," Ramya declared. "That's the plan for now."

"Hmm," said the captain. For a long, quiet while, they sat looking at things other than each other. Then the captain cleared his throat. "Well, I wish I could take you there, but the *Endeavor* is not equipped that well. The Fringe is full of pirates and many other unpleasant creatures, and this old ship will be like a sitting duck out there."

"I know," Ramya said quickly to assure him that she was not expecting him to help her all the way to the Fringe. "I'll find another transport from somewhere near the outer settlements. You can drop me off wherever you think is best."

The captain's eyes clouded; whether it was fear or concern for her or both, Ramya didn't know.

"Anyway, we need to sort out this trouble with the Stryker first before anyone goes anywhere," she added.

The captain looked away, his tone gruff when he spoke again. "The Fringe is not an easy or safe place to be, especially not for you, Lady Ramya Kiroff."

His words felt like a slap. It stung like nothing before. Not even her father's habitual derision pained her as much. Ramya felt her eyes burn and her sight blur. She blinked, fast and furious, determined not to let her hurt show. She also wondered what had upset her so much. Was it the thought that it'd be hard for her to survive the Fringe, or was it because of the formal address he used? It was more of the latter, she decided.

Gulping to drive away that ache in her throat, Ramya found a few words and she uttered them out as firmly as she could. "Please don't call me that, Captain. I don't want to hear that name."

Ramya saw the captain's jaw tighten, but before the ripples on his forehead could deepen, a sharp rap sounded on the door. Ramya jumped at the interruption, almost spilling what remained of the noja in her cup.

"Yes," hollered the captain.

"It's me, Captain. Fenny."

"Come in."

The petite navigator of the *Endeavor* walked in with a sullen face. She barely glanced at Ramya, instead keeping her gaze locked on the captain.

"Ross is in the COM with Wiz, and they seem to be doing fine by themselves," Fenny informed. "I'm going to go back to the cargo bay. The Pterostrich cage needs some mending, so I thought now's a good time to take care of that."

Captain Milos nodded. "All right. Go. Take Rami with you."

Fenny flinched at his words and shook her head with vehemence. "I don't need her, Captain," she said in a scathing tone, throwing an annoyed sidelong glance at Ramya.

The captain raised an eyebrow and Ramya wondered what could be wrong. Fenny had always been friendly with her.

"I'll be fine on my own, Captain," Fenny said again as the captain continued to stare. "Rami can be with Sosa. I'm sure she'll be needed there."

Refusing help, particularly with mending the Pterostrich cage, was weird. Fenny wasn't cursing anymore either, which Ramya thought was extremely odd.

"You're taking her with you, Fenny." The captain's order was crisp with an air of finality.

Fenny nodded, but it was clearly a grudging consent. Then, without even acknowledging Ramya, the woman marched out of the captain's room.

17

Ramya had to rush to catch up with Fenny who strode away without sparing her a glance. "Fenny," Ramya yelled, trying to wrestle some attention from the woman. "Wait."

Fenny didn't stop until she was in the elevator. Even then, she refused to look at Ramya and simply stared at the ceiling grim-faced.

"What's wrong?" Ramya demanded. She had always found Fenny to be a cheerful, if loud, presence. The Fenny of now was not normal. Had something happened between her and the others? Could Ross have said something to make her mad? He had been with her in the cargo bay, and although Ramya hadn't noticed them squabbling in the feed, they could've fought later.

"Fenny?" Ramya tried again. "Why aren't you talking to me?"

"Not in the mood," Fenny snapped. The elevator screeched to a halt and Fenny darted out of it as if staying there a second longer would burn her.

Ramya followed her out and they walked silently to the weapons storage. Fenny picked two blasters and handed one to Ramya. She also picked some armor and gave Ramya one. As soon as they had finished donning their helmets, Fenny stomped out of the weapons cache and back into the elevator.

Ramya confronted the woman when the doors closed. "All right, Fenny," she started, "you need to tell me what's going on. Tell me right now, or—"

"Or what?" Fenny almost spat. She took a step toward Ramya and glared. "What are you gonna do to me, Lady Ramya Kiroff? Blast me out of the iffin galaxy?"

Ramya fell back a step, stunned by Fenny's vicious response even before the meaning of Fenny's words dawned on her. It was not until the doors of the elevator opened once more and she had followed Fenny out to the entrance of the cargo hold that Ramya could speak.

"Wait. Did you just call me Lady Ramya Kiroff? How do you . . . you know . . ." Ramya's words faded midway, a million thoughts bombarding her mind. Fenny had to have overheard the captain addressing her as "lady." And Fenny wasn't angry with Ross, but with her. "Oh, come on, Fenny," Ramya pleaded. "What are you so mad about?"

Fenny was busily punching in the entrance code at the door of the hold, but she stopped and whirled around to face Ramya. "Why am I mad? Well, because you iffin lied to me, that's why," she yelled, and jabbed an accusing finger in the air. "I thought you were a poor, little motherless kid, and I cared about you and . . . trusted you. I fought with Ross because of you. And you? You've been playing me . . . us all the while."

"Well, I'm sorry, but I didn't have a choice, Fenny," Ramya protested. "I'm not on a vacation, I'm on the run. I couldn't simply tell you who I wa—"

"Stop," Fenny said. She held her arms up and hissed, "Just stop. I don't know what wool you've managed to pull over the captain's eyes, but do *not* try to convince me you're all innocent, all right? I know who you are and what you are now."

Ramya's throat was quickly filling up with hurt, but she managed a whisper. "You do? So tell me then, who am I?"

Fenny placed her hands on her hips and simply heaved for a while before she uttered a sound. "You're a spoiled little rich kid who has lied her way into my ship and is going to cause everyone I love and care about a whole lot of trouble." She gritted her teeth and paused a while, as if to stop the rest of her cruel words from spilling out. "You're a selfish brat whose whim for adventure might get all of us killed."

Raw anger burned in Fenny's eyes and along with it the swirling hatred. How could Fenny hate her that much? She had only hidden her identity, not harmed anyone. And Fenny thought Ramya was *running away* because she had a *whim for adventure*? Ramya couldn't bear to look at Fenny's raging face anymore so she turned away. Besides, she also needed to quietly blink away the tears she knew were about to slip past her barricades.

"Now you're going to turn away," Fenny said, sarcasm dripping from her voice. "Well, that won't change anything. You'll still be a two-bit liar, just like your father."

Ramya took in a long, deep breath. She was nothing like her father. She could never be anything like her father. And Fenny needed to know that. Ramya passed a hand over her still-moist eyes and turned around slowly.

"Call me whatever you want to call me, Fenny, but do not compare me to my father. Not now, not ever. Do you understand?"

Ramya realized she had spoken too harshly from the way Fenny's eyes narrowed and nostrils flared. The woman recovered quickly though. Crossing her arms, she tilted a stubborn chin in Ramya's direction.

"And why shouldn't I?" Fenny asked. "Runaway or not, you're still his daughter and heiress to his endless fortune, aren't you?"

"As if I care about his fortune. I'd take this ship over Somenvaar any day."

Fenny froze and then she blinked and frowned before throwing her arms up in the air. "All right, that's it. I can't pretend like I'm not curious to know. Have you lost it? Are you seriously leaving it all behind?"

Ramya couldn't help but roll her eyes. She knew it probably looked juvenile and immature and so much like Isbet, but she couldn't stop it. What did Fenny think she was doing, playing hide-and-seek with her father?

"Yes, quite seriously," she said. "You have no idea what my father would do if he got his hands on me."

"Will he disown you?"

Ramya scoffed. "That would have been good. But he won't. I was born into the Kiroff family so he'll always find a use for me. But along the way he'll humiliate me in the worst way possible and then some."

"But why?" Fenny asked. "You're his daughter. He must care about you."

"He gives a damn about me."

Fenny scrunched her shoulders, indignant. Ramya knew that disbelieving look in Fenny's eyes. Isbet always gave her the same look. No one believed how much her father disliked her. No one.

Ramya pushed down a sigh. This wasn't the time for self-pity. "He always wanted a male heir, but got me instead," she said. "I'm this worthless girl who is not outstanding at anything. At CAWStrat my father got trophies for everything he participated in. And I? The best I could muster in two years was an honorable mention. Heck, I'm not even a beauty."

Fenny's face had been dimming steadily as she listened to Ramya. Now she made a face. "Who said you aren't pretty?"

"My father. All my life," Ramya replied, chuckling. She remembered the first time she had heard him say it. She must've been five or six. "An ugly mutt of girl" he had called her. She had cried for weeks and never told anyone about it, not even to Isbet. Yet now it felt strangely liberating to tell Fenny. "He has always called me ugly. Well, it's true I am nothing compared to my mother. She's —"

Fenny's mouth twisted as she scoffed. "I don't know about anyone else, but my vote is with you. Besides, who cares about looks anyway? You're a sharp kid, and that's all that matters."

"Hah! You should tell my father that. He'll find it quite funny."

Fenny balked. "Why is that? You *are* plenty smart. You snuck out of . . . wherever and got in here. Iffin Trysten hasn't found you yet, has he? Then you fought that bird. And you helped Sosa. Heck, you even helped out in the COM. If that's not smart I don't know what is."

Ramya let out a long sigh. "Like I said, go tell that to my father. The only use he has for me is as bait, to lure another family into a marriage alliance. Then he'd train the man I marry to be his real successor. That's his grand plan for me."

"Seriously?"

"Yes, Fenny. Seriously. He was about to pull me out of the CAWStrat and get me married to some random guy. That's when I ran."

"So that's why."

"Yes, that's why. It wasn't just a whim."

"Hey, the jury's still out on that. If you ask me, the situation doesn't sound that awful anyway. Sure, Trysten Kiroff is a pig, but I don't see how marrying a guy he picked for you would be a bad thing. I mean, that guy would also have to be iffin rich to begin with for your father to choose him. You'd have a nice little life and not be fighting stinky hatchlings on a rundown ship."

It was Ramya's turn to shake her head. "Really? That guy would probably be just as slimy as my father. And he'd be marrying me for my father's money. What would that make me?"

"Hmm, I don't know." Fenny thoughtfully rubbed her nose. "What would it make you? A wife maybe? One he'd move the heavens to please?"

Ramya stifled a sigh. "Please me? More like please my father."

"Ah." Fenny nodded like a wise sage. "So, the girl wants to marry for love, huh?" Fenny said in a singsong voice. "She wants to find her prince charming on her own."

"Oh, shut up," Ramya retorted, and Fenny broke into noisy cackles.

Ramya felt her face grow warmer. What was wrong with looking for love? That wasn't asking for much.

Fenny patted Ramya's shoulder. "All right, sister. That's enough chitchat for now. Back to work." She turned back to face the door. "Your ladyship needs to learn to clean some bird poop."

"Wait! What?"

Fenny vigorously punched the buttons of the door lock. "We have to clean the cage because the whole cargo bay smells like shit. We have to feed the chick again and extend the cage so she has enough room as she grows."

"It's a she?" Ramya asked, squinting at Fenny.

Fenny shrugged. "Yes, Vittoria is a girl."

Ramya took more than a second to react to that. "Vittoria?" she said, blinking.

"Don't you like the name?"

"That's not the point. Why would you name a murderous bird? It's bad enough we're keeping it alive, and now . . ."

Fenny face drooped a little. "It's not Vittoria's fault that she hatched on the *Endeavor*. It's ours. We destroyed her life. None of the other eggs are hatching either, poor things. I think they're all dead."

Good riddance, Ramya thought. She didn't say it aloud though. Seeing Fenny's downcast eyes, she didn't have the heart to.

"So how long do you think we'll be serving Queen Vittoria?" she asked, and Fenny chucked loudly.

"I'd say we have a few hours of work cut out for us." She paused and shot a teasing look at Ramya. "Still think it was a good idea to run?"

"Yes, a hundred times yes," Ramya replied without hesitation. If someone were to rewind time back to that moment when she decided to sneak out of the CAWStrat and ask her if she'd to do it all over again, she would pick this path to the *Endeavor* without a second thought.

Fenny flashed a smile and shook her head a little. "Well, come on then. Let's get to work."

18

Cleaning the Pterostrich cage was tiring and dirty work, no doubt about that. The only thing that kept Ramya going through the task was knowing that Fenny had softened. Even if she had not forgiven Ramya completely, at least the cheerful and talkative Fenny was back. After the cleaning was complete, they built an extension to the cage. Hours passed at a jaunty pace. Fenny shared a zillion tales about the *Endeavor* and its eclectic crew from the time she was recruited five years ago.

"I was a shuttle mechanic on Alameda," she said as they fit the pieces of thick wire frames onto the cage. "One day the captain came by my workshop looking for someone to fix a kink in the impulse engine, so I went. The *Endeavor* was a pile of junk back then, and the captain had just purchased it from the traders up north. It was one of the battered battleships the Confederacy discarded after the Locusta-Vanga war. So, anyway, I fixed it for him. He told me he was looking for a crew and if I knew anyone who'd be interested in running a freight op with him on the *Endeavor*."

"And you jumped at it?" Ramya asked.

Fenny shrugged. "Sort of. Wanted to fly around the galaxy all my life. Never had enough money, never went to school either, so I figured that was my best chance to get off the iffin cute prime planet. I'd always stuck out like a sore thumb on it anyway. Didn't miss it much."

"How about family?" Ramya asked, regretting immediately that she did. She didn't have to go nosing around. If Fenny had family she'd have said that already.

"Nope," Fenny said. "Never knew my parents. Was raised in an orphanage. They kicked me out when I was fifteen and I found work at that shuttle repair shop. It wasn't a bad place if you knew how to take care of yourself."

"So you were the first recruit," Ramya said.

Fenny chuckled as they fit the extension they had built to the existing frame of the cage.

"Yes, I was," she said. "We ran into Wiz two days later. Flew out of Alameda soon after."

Ramya was about to ask when Sosa joined the crew. The Norgoran had spoken about knowing Captain Milos for over twenty years, but if the captain only started recruiting for the *Endeavor* five years ago, they must've known each other from before then.

Just then, the Pterostrich chick sat up suddenly and craned its long neck, peering one way and then another. It had been resting in the far corner of the cage after having stuffed itself full of the sedative-sprinkled meat Fenny and Ramya had served. From time to time, it opened its large yellow eyes and looked as they worked on the other end of the cage.

Fenny stopped driving the final set of screws into the cage frame and squinted worriedly at the bird. "What's up with Vi?" she muttered.

Ramya had taken her hands off the cage and she pulled her blaster close. There was no trusting a Pterostrich, half-sedated or otherwise.

"Something's scared it," Ramya whispered, inching a tad toward Fenny. The bird blinked rapidly, the sparse feather on its neck standing out like barbs. It tried to stand up but its legs buckled. Ramya let go of the breath she had been holding. *Thank goodness the tranquilizer still had some effect.*

"What the hell?" Fenny muttered. She looked around the cargo hold, craning her neck as much as she could, as did Ramya. There was nothing odd. All around them the cargo bay was quiet and still. Nothing moved, nothing creaked.

"It's probably nothing," Ramya said. She looked askance at the chick. It also seemed less nervous now. The feathers had fallen flat against its neck and it didn't blink as rapidly. Whatever had bothered it had possibly passed.

"Let's get this done and get out of here," Fenny said, her brows furrowed deep.

Ramya couldn't agree more. The cargo hold gave her the creeps, and the memory of the Pterostrich attack didn't help any either. The sooner she could get out of there the better. She rushed, fastening bolts into the wire frame at a rapid pace. They were done with the construction within a few more minutes. Ramya and Fenny tugged and pulled at the joints to make sure it was sturdy and then they removed the partition between the old cage and the new. The chick simply opened its eyes once and promptly curled up some more.

"What? You aren't even gonna look?" Fenny cocked her head at the chick and said in mock anger. "We added a brand new room to your house and you still aren't happy?"

"We might've as well saved two hours of our life, Fenny."

"You're right." Fenny crossed her arms and shook her head. "A real queen she is."

Ramya chuckled as she packed up the equipment. "You've given her too much of the sleep drug, Fenny," she said. "Once that wears off, she'll be thanking you."

"Thankless featherbrain," Fenny grumbled on.

Laughing, Ramya was about to pick up the crate of equipment, when she froze. It was barely there, but the floor was unmistakably shaking under her feet. "Fenny," she called. "You feel that?"

The hum sounded before Fenny could answer. It was a buzzing sound, reminding Ramya of flying insects during summers at Somenvaar, only sharper and more intense.

Fenny stood still for a second before she jutted her lower lip out. Then she froze. "Oh no, not that again!"

Chill coursed up Ramya's spine. "What do you mean?"

"The Stryker," Fenny whispered. "It was doing the same thing when we were camped next to it waiting for the GSO."

"You mean the Stryker's making this weird vibration?" Ramya asked hesitantly.

"Seems like it." Fenny let out a long breath. "It was barely for a few seconds though. We couldn't be entirely sure," she replied in a low voice.

The vibration grew stronger under their feet and the hum rose to a higher pitch.

"Perhaps we should check it out," Fenny muttered.

"Check it out?" Ramya asked. She was not dying to quench her curiosity. Although checking it out was the logical thing to do. They were here, in the hold and in position to investigate the disturbance, so why delay?

Fenny bit her lip and frowned. Her finger hovered over the button of her comm for a second or two before she pressed it hard. All that came out of it was a loud buzz.

"What the iffin hell?" Fenny said. She pressed the button a few more times. Off and on. Off and on again. Each time the loud buzz greeted them.

"Something's wrong with the channel?" Ramya asked, and Fenny shrugged in response.

"Damn you, Flux." Fenny slapped the button another time. Clearly Flux had yet another issue on his hands. The *Endeavor* was surely good at keeping the engineer busy.

Ramya grabbed the woman's arm and nudged her. "Fenny," she said. "Let's go and get a few more people."

It seemed that Fenny was torn between investigating and leaving the hold right away as Ramya suggested. She raised an eyebrow at Ramya. "We don't have that many people. Let's check it out quickly. Then we can get out of here and report to the captain."

"All right," Ramya said grudgingly after a bit. "Let's go take a quick look."

Ramya's insides puckered as they took the first step toward the far end of the cargo hold. She gripped her blaster tighter, her senses on alert as they drew closer to the Stryker.

A humming Stryker or not, the situation was far better than the last time she was in here, Ramya had to admit. It had been pitch-dark then, and cold. Now at least they could see if someone was lurking around. Her heart thudded louder as she recalled what Captain Milos had said—the Locustan ships were thought to be biomechanical. And if this Stryker had Locustan tech embedded in it, would that mean it too was biomechanical? Was the ship alive? Or sentient?

"Rami . . ." Fenny's sharp whisper brought Ramya's thoughts to a skidding halt. "Do you see that?"

The Point Masks they had fitted all over the body of the Stryker to create a cloak of invisibility over the ship shielded almost the entire Stryker except for the nose and a bit of the body behind it where the masks didn't work. That was the only part of the Stryker that was visible now, and the entire section was covered in a strange reddish glow that pulsed, slowly and gently, like an emergency beacon. A shudder streaked up Ramya's spine and shook her. The sight was downright creepy—the sharp, long nose that was menacing to begin with was made a hundred times creepier with the red glow.

"Why is it doing that?" Ramya blurted, knowing well Fenny didn't know the answer either.

"Wait," Fenny said, and rushed away to one side of the Stryker. She turned off the power supply to the Point Masks and in an instant the entire Stryker—all of it pulsing red—became visible.

Fenny stepped closer to the Stryker, and Ramya inched forward also. Other than the glowing and humming and looking monstrous, the ship seemed harmless. Fenny approached the midsection of the craft and stopped. Once again she punched the red button on her comm only to be greeted by the uncooperative buzz of a blocked communication channel. Fenny's lips curled and she spat out a curse. Ramya threw a quick glance around. Except for the Stryker, everything was calm and quiet, and there was nothing odd in the cargo bay.

Fenny was eyeing the faint oval outline of the Stryker's doorway when Ramya walked over. "An alarm could've gone off, don't you think?" Fenny whispered. "I don't see anything strange here. The door is closed just like it was after we dragged that pilot out."

Fenny nudged the gleaming surface of the door with the muzzle of her blaster, gently at first and then with a little more force. Nothing budged. "See?" she said. "It's closed."

Ramya didn't know what to say. Fenny was correct, there seemed nothing wrong with the Stryker. "The captain might know something," she said. "Let's go back and tell him."

"Let's check one last time," Fenny said. She pulled out a collapsible step from one of the shelves and placed it next to the Stryker's door. Then climbing up to the topmost step, Fenny placed the hefty stock of her blaster against the door and gave it a push. Hoping to aid Fenny with a shove, Ramya placed her hand on the door.

Without warning, the door of the ship slid open with a groan and Fenny screamed as she fell into the Stryker. Ramya froze, watching Fenny careen headfirst into the dimly lit interior of the Stryker.

"Fenny," Ramya yelled in a panic. She clambered up the steps and jumped into the belly of the Stryker. Fear tap-danced at the base of her spine and a wave of nausea filled her stomach and traveled up her throat as she fell into the unknown. She landed with a hefty thud on a hard surface, her heart pounding against her ribs at a maddening pace. Fenny was beside her, scrambling to a sitting position. "Are you all right?" Ramya grasped Fenny by her shoulders and looked into her eyes.

With a loud slam, the door above them closed.

"The door," Fenny yelled, and Ramya dived immediately to keep it open, but it was no use. She ran her hand over the cold surface inlaid with an exotic design of knots that reminded Maia of sinewy muscles and tissue. There was no lever she could press to open it again. There was nothing—no depressions, no hinges, and no handles to pull at all.

Ramya stared at the door and panted. She felt Fenny inch closer behind her. "We're stuck, aren't we?" Fenny said in a breathless voice.

Ramya nodded. Her guts clenched, fear forming a tight ball at its bottom. She turned toward Fenny slowly and saw the same fear reflected in her crewmate's dark wide eyes.

"W-what are we going to do?" Ramya stuttered.

Fenny pushed the door a few times and then the button of her comm. Nothing happened, nothing to bring a smidgeon of cheer to them. The two sat side by side for a long while, Ramya's mind spinning thoughtlessly in endless cycles until a realization brought it to a sudden stop.

"Fenny, the humming," she cried. "I don't hear the humming anymore."

"You're right," Fenny said. "That's gone. But what's the difference? We're here, stuck for who knows how long."

"They'll realize we're missing," Ramya said reassuringly. "Someone will come to check soon."

"And how do you think they'll get us out?" Fenny demanded.

Ramya closed her eyes and breathed in deep. Even though fear was weighing her down, she knew she couldn't let it. They had to find a way out of this thing, and falling apart with fear and panic wasn't going to make that happen. Ramya clutched her blaster and rose to her feet.

"Fenny," she said, forcing as much conviction as she could muster into her voice. "Let's check this thing. There has to be something here we can use to get out."

Fenny tightened her lips and didn't seem even a tad convinced. But she nodded nonetheless. In the next second, she was standing next to Ramya, blaster held tightly in her hands. They were in a sizeable alcove of sorts, shaped like an ovoid. It was almost as if they were inside an egg. To the left of where they stood was a door that led to the front of the ship, Ramya assumed. There was another opening to their right which had to lead to the tail section. Smack dab at the center of the egg-shaped area was a pedestal with a glass container that held a sphere.

Ramya pointed at the pedestal. "What could that be?"

"No idea," Fenny said, shrugging. "Let's take a look. What more could go wrong anyway?"

A lot more can go wrong, Ramya thought. They were being held captive by a strange ship infused with Locustan tech, so there were a million ways things could get even worse from here. But their situation was not about to improve by sitting quietly in a corner either.

Three steps and they were facing the pedestal. Its base was made from a whitish metal with a pink tinge that covered the rest of the ship's interior. All over it were intricate patterns. The sphere atop it was different. It was dark like the ship's exterior, and its surface ridged and wavy. It reminded Ramya of a brain, only this brain was a perfect sphere.

"I see some notches here," Fenny said, running a finger over a series of slim protrusions on the side of the pedestal. Fenny's touch didn't make a difference, but Ramya was curious for a feel. She placed a finger on the leftmost protrusion and drew a line across them. She couldn't be sure, but it felt like the ridges trembled under her touch.

"Did you feel that, Fe—"

The rest of Ramya's words were lost in the confusion that followed. Lights flashed, Ramya and Fenny fell back in alarm, and the sphere inside the glass container atop the pedestal glowed a bright green and levitated.

19

For moments that seemed to stretch forever, the only thing Ramya could be sure of was the beating of her heart as it thrashed wildly against her ribs. The rest was a blur until a soft, childish voice filled the ovoid with its crisp sweetness.

"Took you a long time to get here, Mihaal," it said, almost giggling. With every word uttered, the sphere blinked. "Dakrhaeth has been waiting."

Ramya exchanged a quick, confused glance with Fenny. *Who was that? What in the stars did it mean?*

"Who . . . I mean . . . what are you?" Ramya barely managed to stutter.

"It's an AI," Fenny whispered. "An artificial intelligence. All newer Confederacy ships have those installed." She paused and muttered, "I hate them."

"Dakrhaeth is not an AI," the voice retorted, making Ramya stiffen. Fenny had barely whispered and he . . . it had heard her? The voice continued, somewhat peevishly. "Dakrhaeth is far more than your AIs could be. Dakrhaeth is the soul of this ship."

"I see," Ramya replied, although she didn't really see or understand much. But this much she knew: if they were standing in the thing's belly it was probably not a good idea to rile it.

"I don't get the difference," Fenny whispered in her ear.

"The difference can wait," Ramya muttered through gritted teeth. All they needed now was to get out of here. "Why did you wake up all of a sudden?" she asked the sphere.

"You touched Dakrhaeth. Dakrhaeth had to wake up. Dakrhaeth is *your* ship after all," it said. Ramya thought she could detect a hint of happiness in the strange voice.

"My ship?" Ramya asked, gaping. "You're not *my* ship."

"Of course I am. You're the one who resurrected Dakrhaeth," the voice insisted. "The rider you assigned Dakrhaeth has faded. Until you pair Dakrhaeth with a new rider, Dakrhaeth is yours. That's how Virikhshis work."

"Whoa," Fenny said. "Virikhshis? That's what they called a Locustan ship. Why the hell would . . ." her words faded. Fenny eyes grew large and fearful, and Ramya realized that Fenny wasn't aware of the conversation she'd had with the dying pilot or the one she'd had subsequently with Ross and Captain Milos. Fenny didn't know that this ship, the Stryker, had Locustan tech embedded in it.

"Dakrhaeth is a Viriskshi," the voice informed. "Or he used to be one. Dakrhaeth crashed along with his squadron on a planet you, of the Confederacy, call the Kyo-Sedra-5."

"No way," Fenny muttered, her disbelieving tone quickly turning to annoyed. "Don't tell me that iffin Kiroff was experimenting with Locustan tech."

The voice went on with its startling crispness. "Dakrhaeth lay there, half buried in the planet's ice, damaged and immobile, until you came and resurrected Dakrhaeth and a few of the other riders."

Ramya held up her hands. This was getting too crazy. "I did *not* resurrect you or any others. I've never been on Kyo-Sedra-5 or even in Sector 22."

"Dakrhaeth recognizes you, Mihaal," the voice insisted. "You have the same essence as the one Dakrhaeth gazed upon when he came to life again. You're the one who got us all new bodies. You're the one who made Dakrhaeth live again."

"Well, congratulations, Rami," Fenny whispered. "You have a new baby."

Ramya flashed an annoyed look at the woman and then frowned at the sphere. She decided to take a different route.

"Why do you keep calling me Mihaal? What does that even mean?"

"In Dakrhaeth's own tongue, it means 'the creator,'" the sphere said. It was slowly spinning around inside the glass container as it spoke, and it continued to glow with a creepy green light.

Fenny chuckled. "Congratulations, Rami, you're his God," she said.

"Fenny, I've never even seen this thing before," Ramya whispered.

"I think . . ." — Fenny shot a wary look at Ramya — "I think it's mistaken you for your father."

"What?" Ramya blurted. A frozen moment passed, and then another until she realized what Fenny said made sense. The Stryker had detected her presence and let her in because it thought she was Trysten Kiroff. "You think it ran some biometric scan?"

Fenny shrugged. "Would be logical to have one."

"But I'm not him."

"Of course. But maybe the scanning isn't flawless yet. They were still testing these things in their factory, remember?"

Indeed. Fenny had a point, a good one.

Fenny nudged her arm. "Hey, Rami, why don't you ask your minion to set us free?"

"Yes, I will," Ramya replied. That was her plan, to get the sphere to open the door. The captain or the Confederacy could talk to it later if they wanted. All she wanted was to get out of here.

Ramya took a step closer to the pedestal and smiled, although she didn't know if a smile meant anything to the ship or if it even saw her smile.

"Um . . . Dakrhaeth," she started hesitantly, "can you please open the door so we can get out? I'll come back later to talk to you." That was a lie through and through; Ramya had no intention of getting back inside this creepy Stryker again.

"Dakrhaeth can and he will since you've asked," the ship replied. "But Dakrhaeth thinks you should stay and hear what he has to say before you go report to your captain."

How did it know that they were going to report to the captain? Was it reading her mind? She felt Fenny shuffle next to her.

"What is it?" Ramya said, keeping her voice steady and face straight.

"Dakrhaeth came to your world from another—a dark one, far, far away, deep in the Mehulian Quadrant. Dakrhaeth's world wants to devour yours and many more. That's our way of life."

He was talking about the Locustans, Ramya deduced. But why was he telling them all that? Somewhere in the pit of her stomach, fear raised an uneasy head.

"Your people resisted Dakrhaeth and his rider and all other riders who flew with us. You were brave, but mostly . . . lucky."

Next to Ramya, Fenny fidgeted. Ramya herself struggled to stop herself from retorting. Luck had nothing to do with their winning the Locusta-Vanga war; the Confederacy had fought back the Locustans with all they had. People like Grappa gave his life fighting the scourge, Captain Milos risked his. That wasn't luck. It was bravery and sacrifice and outwitting the bane that was the Locustans. But now wasn't the time to argue with a crazy AI, so she waited for it to say more.

"But this time, luck won't be on your side," Dakrhaeth declared. "The others you resurrected along with Dakrhaeth are out to destroy the Fringe colonies as we speak. They're laying the groundwork for the second invasion to begin. A pathway to the dark world Dakrhaeth came from is about to open up soon, and riders—far numerous than you've seen before—will come and consume your world."

Ramya couldn't take it anymore. "All right," she said. "We've heard enough of your doomsday talk. We have to leave. So please open the door."

"Dakrhaeth maybe young, but he's intelligent," said the voice. "You'd be wise to heed his words."

What a narcissistic spawn of the devil! Ramya gritted her teeth as her fists clenched. Half of her wanted to slam a fist against that glass container, yet the other half knew she had to keep calm.

"What do you suggest we do?" Fenny asked brightly, much to Ramya's relief.

"Warn your leaders," Dakrhaeth replied. "Tell them they shouldn't waste time trying to destroy Dakrhaeth. He is not what they should be worried about. They should instead look for the ones that have gone missing."

"Wait a second," Ramya blurted. "How do you know they're worried about you?"

"Dakrhaeth is wise, he knows."

His vanity grated her endlessly, but Ramya had to keep the communication lines open. She still didn't quite understand what this creepy AI was up to. "It seems to me that you're trying to help us, but I don't understand why. Why didn't you join the rest of your buddies in helping with the next invasion?"

For a second or two, a nervous silence hung in the chamber. Then the sphere spoke again. "You gave Dakrhaeth his life back, he's grateful."

There seemed to be something else that remained unspoken and Ramya felt a hesitation turn the air heavy. She was about to ask, but at that precise moment, the door slid open behind them.

Fenny jumped out before Ramya could blink. "Come on, Rami," she yelled.

Ramya had taken a step backward when the sphere blinked again. "Dakrhaeth doesn't wish to die again. And that's what Admiral Kanaa has planned for him and for all of you when you reach Alameda."

"How do you know about Admiral Kanaa? How—"

"Dakrhaeth heard that the derelict—*Endeavor*, pardon the slip— was headed to Alameda. And Dakrhaeth knows there's one person in Alameda who will want to make sure he's dead."

"Rami," Fenny yelled. "We have to go. Get out of there, please."

"Mihaal, Admiral Kanaa will not wait to extract Dakrhaeth from the *Endeavor* so she can destroy only him. She will not even wait to extract you from the *Endeavor*. She will fire at will to destroy everything — the *Endeavor*, you, and Dakrhaeth."

Ramya stared at the slowly spinning orb in disbelief. That couldn't be. The top officer of the Confederate Space Command wouldn't just fire at the *Endeavor* and destroy everything inside it. Besides, the *Endeavor* belonged to Captain Milos, they just couldn't—

"Rami," Fenny yelled again.

"Yes, I'm coming," Ramya shouted back. She had to go, but she couldn't ignore what this sphere, Dakrhaeth, had just told them. His talk was pretentious, but didn't sound crazy. There was much more to it and she had a feeling that the captain would agree.

20

For the third time that day, Ramya found herself sitting in the captain's room across from a sullen Terenze Milos who was growing gruffer by the second. As soon as she had returned with Fenny and reported on the Stryker's AI, the captain had ordered her to take a seat and dispatched Fenny to Engineering to help Flux fix the issue with the communication channels.

"You will stay here," the captain had instructed after Fenny left. "Drink some noja, read a book, take a nap, but do not leave this room." With that, he too had left. As much as Ramya had wanted to sneak out and find out what was happening, she could not bring herself to ignore the captain's direct order, so she stayed put. She had picked a book on galactic history from the bookshelf and curled up with it on a couch.

After what seemed like an eternity, the door opened and the captain walked in. He pulled up a chair and squinted hard at her.

"Rami, I need you to listen to me very carefully," he said. "And I need you to be very brave and follow my orders without asking any questions. Can you do that?"

"Yes," Ramya replied, nodding vigorously. Of course she could do that. She'd do whatever was needed of her.

"We're about to make contact with the Confederacy soon. Not at Alameda, but at Totori. Do you know anything about Totori?"

Ramya shook her head. She'd heard that name, but it wasn't as significant a place that she'd remember right away.

"Let me tell you about Totori," said the captain. "It's the star system nearest to Alameda's. The best thing about Totori is the location of the AP—it's right next to an asteroid belt."

"I remember," Ramya blurted. She suddenly recalled what she

had read about Totori in her Galactic Economics book. Totori was a mining haven. That was not because the planets were rich in minerals, but because of its proximity to the mineral-rich Noxillian Asteroid Belt or the NAB as the Confederacy dubbed it.

"In case what our friend down in the cargo bay told you is true, we'll need an escape plan. And the asteroid belt can be a—"

"Shield?" Ramya interjected and immediately muttered an apology.

The captain waved her apology away. "You're right. It could be a natural barrier for us in case of an assault."

Ramya stiffened at his words.

"You think there's a possibility of an attack? You believe that AI? It's Locustan. It could be setting us up," she said. Captain Milos frowned and pursed his lips. He was the captain of the *Endeavor*, her captain and superior, and grilling him about his judgment was against every protocol. But even though Ramya thought about it, she felt no qualms about questioning Captain Milos. She knew he wouldn't mind, and even if he did, she wouldn't resent being reprimanded. In plain and simple words, Ramya had grown to trust him. Calmly, she went on. "Do you really think the Confederacy would fire on the *Endeavor* knowing we're in it? Really?"

The captain's gaze darted to the floor for a brief second. Then they came back to meet hers. "I'm not sure, Rami," he said. "All I know is I have to be prepared."

"But you've known Admiral Kanaa," Ramya said. "Would she do that to *you*?"

"People find their reasons for doing things, Rami." The captain sighed. "When someone thinks the truth they know is the one and only truth, it can be very hard to make them understand otherwise."

Ramya thought she understood what the captain meant even though she could not fathom why he said that. Did he mean that about Kanaa, or was it just a random snippet of wisdom?

"Anyway, I'm hoping we won't have to meet the admiral,"

Captain Milos said before Ramya could come to a conclusion about his previous comment.

Ramya didn't understand. Weren't they supposed to deliver the Stryker to the Confederacy? "How will you give them the Stryker then?" she asked.

"We're going to drop it off on an asteroid."

Ramya sat up. So that was the plan, avoid contacting the Confederacy until the *Endeavor* was out of reach and safe.

"They can come and pick it up after we've left," the captain said.

Somehow the thought of leaving the fighter alone on a drifting space rock made Ramya uneasy. There was no logical reason to feel this way, yet . . .

"You need to visit the Stryker one more time. Ross will be with you," Captain Milos informed.

Ramya winced. Why did she need to go? Then there was the mention of the commander's name. Why couldn't Fenny come with her instead?

"Anything wrong?" the captain asked.

"No," Ramya lied. Now was not the time for petty rows. "What will we do there?"

"Wait for my orders."

"What kind of order?"

A ghost of a smile flitted across the captain's weathered face. "You'll find out when it's time."

Not at all satisfied with that answer, Ramya was about to probe some more but the door opened behind them and Ross peeked in. "I'm ready, Captain," he said. "Got everything I need."

The captain nodded at him and looked at Ramya. "Off you go now. You'll assist the commander during the Stryker's transfer."

"You know the Confederacy will possibly destroy the Stryker, right?" Ramya asked as she rose to her feet. "You're still going to give it away?"

"If they want it, then yes, of course," replied the captain. "Now go."

***

A few minutes later, Ramya was hunkered down with Ross on a bench next to the Stryker. Things were a little different this time. Ross had activated a partition in the hold where the Stryker had been sitting, which he said was the air lock. The hatch that'd be opened during the transfer of the Stryker was located behind the Stryker's tail end. They were both wearing space suits, although Ross told her she could keep her helmet off until they opened the hatch to deposit the Stryker on an asteroid.

Other than a few instructions, Ross didn't speak much. He kept glancing frequently at the comm on his wrist, impatiently waiting to hear from the captain. Ramya was anxious too, but there was nothing she could do but wait. She didn't even have a comm to speak to anyone else on the ship anyway. Ross replied to her questions with civility and without frowning or scowling too much, and Ramya did not want to push her luck any more. So, she closed her eyes and rested.

Thoughts of the Stryker streamed in the moment her lids shut. That it would soon be given away to Confederacy forces weighed heavily on her heart. For a moment Ramya could not believe she was feeling this way, that she was sad, so sad that her heart wrenched and her throat grew tight.

"They'll kill your Dakrhaeth," she almost heard the Locustan AI saying. That was true. The Confederacy would likely destroy the Stryker. But this wasn't just another ship forged out of metals. This was more—it had a soul. Condemning a living being to certain death for no fault of his wasn't fair.

Ramya's eyes flew open at the sound of a buzz. Ross's comm was blinking, and as soon as he pressed the big red button at its center, the captain's voice filled the hold.

"Commander," the captain said in a tight voice. "Please keep this channel open until the drop is complete."

"Yes, Captain," Ross replied.

"We are exiting the SLH now," the captain added.

Ramya wished she could be in the COM with the captain and Fenny rather than in the cold cargo bay with Ross waiting to give away the Stryker. She wanted to see what was going on outside, how the asteroid belt looked. And she'd rather not be part of the team that sent the Stryker to its death.

"Captain, I see Confederacy ships," Fenny said sharply. "How the hell did they know we'd be here?"

"Ships?" the captain asked. His voice was calm and steady. "How many?"

"I don't iffin believe this," Fenny said. Her voice was loud and rushed, and Ramya knew right away something was very wrong about the situation. Fenny's next words confirmed her fears. "Two Drednots, Captain. One ship has stripes all over."

A lump of fear twisted and turned inside Ramya. This wasn't good. First, the Confederacy was not supposed to know. The captain hadn't even told them they'd be here in Totori. The plan was to not tell the Confederacy until after the *Endeavor* had dropped off the Stryker. How did Admiral Kanaa find out?

Then there was the issue of the Drednots. Drednots were the Confederacy's largest battleships, with firepower second to none. Ramya could recite a standard Drednot's spec even in sleep — four dorsal turrets-mounted ion cannons in pairs in addition to the two plasma-projection cannons on both sides and a third along its center. The plasma cannons were perfect to damage anything unfortunate enough to come near its front. The ion cannons discharged a beam of particles strong enough to rip a vessel apart in seconds. There was no reason for these deadly vessels to be here to welcome the *Endeavor* unless the Confederacy had something extreme on their minds.

"Slow down, Wiz," the captain ordered. "Fenny, hail the admiral.

She should be in that striped flagship, the *Coranthus*."

Moments later, Ramya heard Admiral Kanaa's wheezy voice. "Milos, good to see you after all these years."

"The feeling's mutual, Admiral," the captain replied. "That's quite a welcome party you've arranged for us. Drednots? Am I seeing right?"

"I'm not taking any chances with that rogue ship, Milos," Kanaa replied. "Not until we figure out what monster the Kiroff lab has created that could wipe out an entire GSO fleet."

"I don't think this one had anything to do with that disaster, Admiral," the captain said. "You might want to track down the four other Strykers that have gone missing. They seem to be the ones responsible."

"You let the Confederacy be the judge of that, Milos," the admiral snapped. "Why, may I ask, have you come to Totori? Weren't you supposed to meet us at Alameda?"

"Apologies. We're having slight mechanical issues, Admiral," the captain lied.

"I see. And your approach is quite slow as well. Some trouble with your thrusters, is it?"

"You don't miss anything, Admiral," the captain replied casually. "Let me see if my engineer can speed things up a little. I don't want to keep you waiting."

Admiral Kanaa's reply was bristly. "Don't trouble yourself. I'll ask my ships to move forward."

There was sharp click and Ramya knew what that meant. Admiral Kanaa's channel was either cut off or muted.

"Captain, I just picked up two more Drednots approaching us from behind," Fenny informed breathlessly.

"What the hell?" Wiz said in a panicked tone. "Captain, they're closing in. What should we do?"

"Stay sharp. Prepare for evasive maneuvers," the captain replied.

"Evasive?" Wiz squeaked. "They're approaching us in a ring

formation and they'll have us blocked in from all sides. How will we evade?"

"They're bigger than us, so they'll be less agile," the captain replied steadily. "How far are we from the NAB?"

"Five minutes at least. At full power," Wiz informed.

"Get the shields up," said the captain. "Prepare to run for it at first sign of aggression."

"I say we run now. Four iffin Drednots closing in on us is plenty aggression," Fenny said in a sour tone.

"It's not, Lieutenant," the captain replied. "Commander, are you hearing this?"

"Yes, Captain," Ross said. "We're ready for your orders."

"Good. We're waiting for the first salvo."

Ross drew a sharp breath and stared fixedly at the ceiling. "He's expecting an attack," he muttered. "This isn't good."

"We can fight back, right?" Ramya asked hopefully. The *Endeavor* had a good amount of firepower, it was faster than those behemoth Drednots, and it was close enough to the NAB to take cover. There was a chance, even if slim.

Ross scoffed. "Fight four Drednots? I sure hope Captain Milos can work magic. I've no idea what he's planning."

Ramya stole a glance at the Stryker. The source of all trouble was sitting quietly, its vulturine face lifted up as if studying them.

"Captain," Fenny shouted. "The turrets on the flanking ships are being positioned. They're taking aim at us."

Ramya braced herself. She remembered how the ship had rocked when the GSO's Cutlass had shot its tractor beams on the *Endeavor*. A Drednot's lightest weapon was usually a depleted halfnolium missile.

"Captain, the ships have fired," yelled Fenny.

"Wiz, fall back and head into the NAB," the captain said.

The *Endeavor* tilted sideways, and at the same instant, an ear-splitting blast sounded somewhere near the left side of the ship.

"They're aiming at our left ancillary thruster, Captain," Wiz shouted. "Shield took a hit."

"Just get us to the NAB, Wiz," the captain replied calmly. It was strange that his voice hadn't raised even a notch. "Commander, prepare to board the Stryker."

Ross blinked. "Captain, what do you mean? The Stryker's doors have been closed since—"

"Rami will show you how," said the captain. "Wiz, to the right."

Another blast rocked the *Endeavor* and Ramya would've been knocked right off the bench if Ross hadn't grabbed her by the arm. She had just managed to whisper her thanks when she noticed Ross's glare. "The captain said you'll show me how. What the hell did he mean? How would you know anything about the Stryker?"

"I'll tell you later," Ramya said. It was clear that the captain had not confided in Ross about the AI, but now was not the time to explain. She had no clue what the captain wanted her to do when she got inside the Stryker, but she knew she had to follow his orders. The *Endeavor* swaying nonstop under her feet, Ramya slipped and skidded her way to the Stryker's door.

"Dakrhaeth, open up," Ramya shouted as she knocked.

"What are you doing?" Ross demanded. "Who is—"

The door opened noiselessly revealing the ovoid chamber Ramya had seen earlier. The dark sphere on the pedestal was glowing brighter than before and it kept bobbing up and down in its glass container. Dakrhaeth was undoubtedly excited.

Ramya scrambled in, Ross after her. The door closed behind them.

"You took your time, Mihaal," Dakrhaeth said accusingly.

"Sorry," Ramya blurted. She felt Ross's incredulous stare wavering between the sphere and her back.

"Dakrhaeth didn't expect a response too quickly, Mihaal. It's normal for your kind to take their time," Dakrhaeth said. Ramya gritted her teeth. There it went again, the boastful, arrogant, thing. And to think barely moments ago she was feeling sad to dump it on an asteroid. "The pilot's chamber is to your left," the voice went on.

"There is also room for a co-pilot, if you think your partner is capable of handling the stress."

"What the hell does it think it is?" Ross growled. Ramya stifled a chuckle. Funny that it took him so long to explode.

"Get into the pilot's seat, Ensign," the captain's loud voice blasted over the comm. Clearly he had been listening in on the conversation. "Fenny will open the hatch and let the Stryker drop off the *Endeavor*."

"And then what?" Ross asked. "What are we supposed to do?"

"Use the Stryker to fight back. Find a way to save the *Endeavor*. Try to keep all of us alive," the captain replied simply.

That was, to say the least, a tall order . . . a near impossible order to be honest. But there was no time to dither. Ramya scrambled, breathlessly rushing into the opening to the left of the entry chamber. There were two chairs made of the same dark metal as the sphere that was Dakrhaeth.

"The left seat is yours, Mihaal," Dakrhaeth said.

A barrage of thoughts that should've assailed Ramya long ago came careening through her mind now, leaving her insides in a slushy pile of fear. What in the stars was she doing here? Two years of flight training didn't change the truth. Ramya had blacked out the first time she had flown into space in a scramjet, and this was not even a simple starfighter—it was a biomechanical oddity of a ship with a living, talking Locustan soul inside it. This was no place for her.

"I don't think I can fly this," Ramya said to Ross, her plea only making his stony eyes gleam with anger.

"Too late for that, don't you think?" he hissed.

"Get into the seat, Rami," the captain commanded. "We don't have time. The Drednots have blocked the AP, so we can't get back into the SLH. Now they're chasing us into the asteroid field, blasting every rock in their path."

As if to make his point, the *Endeavor* shook again. A groan of metal—deep and disturbing—reached Ramya's ears. The *Endeavor* didn't stand a chance against four Drednots. But then, she couldn't be the answer, could she?

"Captain, I've no idea how—"

"You don't have to know, Ramya," the captain replied. "If I'm correct then—"

A familiar cloying voice interrupted the captain in its usual self-important way. "Dakrhaeth will show you the way, Mihaal."

As if that was a guarantee of anything.

"Get in, Ramya," Ross said, spitting out her name like it burned his mouth. He was already strapped into the seat to the right of the pilot's chair. "Fenny, open the hatch," he said.

Ramya whispered a small prayer to the stars before sliding into her own seat. She expected it to be cold, but it was surprisingly warm and so pliable that it seemed to mold itself to the contours of her body. Restraints—six of them in all—slid across her torso and held her tight. It was odd how she suddenly felt safe.

The instrument panel flickered and came to life just as Ramya heard the grating of the hatch. She scanned the buttons at a furious pace, trying to understand what each meant. The layout of the panel was similar to a standard Kiroff-manufactured fighter, only larger and with more switches. Ramya quickly identified the basic controls: the flight stick for directional control, the throttle, the launch buttons for the weapons and the like.

A voice sounded reassuringly in her ears. "All you need to do is order, Mihaal. Dakrhaeth do anything you ask, he's is always with you."

Perhaps he was. But Ramya was not going to depend blindly on an AI, and certainly not a Locustan AI.

"Hatch opened," Fenny said on the comm. "Untethering the Stryker now."

"Godspeed, Ro—" The captain's voice broke as the Stryker tumbled out. They fell, out of the lighted insides of the *Endeavor* and into the dimly lit rock-strewn expanse of the Noxillian Asteroid Belt. Panic rose in a tumultuous rush and flapped like a wild bird in

Ramya's chest. She wanted to scream. And run.

Breathe!

It was getting difficult to breathe, but Ramya didn't give up. She had to be brave; she had promised Captain Milos. She had to come through for him and the *Endeavor* and its crew.

"Switch the thrusters on," Dakrhaeth whispered into her ear. How he spoke just to her, she didn't have a clue but she listened nonetheless. Ramya's fingers touched the sleek white button with the red ring.

Keep breathing!

The thrusters on the Stryker came to life and the craft steadied, hovering behind a large asteroid. Ramya felt a movement and she realized the craft was morphing around her. The cockpit slowly rose until she could view all around her. Ramya looked out the windows to assess their situation, realizing suddenly that the improved viewing capability was not something she was thankful for . . . at least not at this moment.

"We're so cooked," Ross said.

Indeed. Ramya had never seen a Drednot up close even though she — like everyone else in the galaxy — had often marveled at the formidable battleship's descriptions in books. But four of them pointing their turrets in her direction didn't seem like the right time for making an acquaintance and certainly not the time to appreciate their beauty or their power.

The Drednots were immense. They looked like they meant business. And right now their business seemed to be wiping the *Endeavor* off the face of the galaxy. The only thing that stood between the behemoths blasting their way through the asteroid field and their puny target was a punier fighter — the Stryker.

"Can you set up a channel to the *Endeavor*?" Ross asked. "It'd be good to talk to the captain."

"No," Dakrhaeth replied in an instant. "Their communication equipment is severely outmoded and out-synched from mine."

"Damn!" Ross muttered. "Keep trying, will ya?"

"I will."

Ross turned and shrugged at Ramya. "Looks like we're on our own."

They were. Orphaned by the *Endeavor*. Alone.

Ramya breathed in deep and stared resolutely at the mammoth Confederacy ships. The more she looked at her outsized foes, the calmer she felt inside. The captain had only tried to do the right thing, and instead of thanking him, the admiral had set these deadly ships loose? This was unfair. This was wrong. Ramya had to make it right. Even though she had little idea of how she was going to take out these giants, there was no doubt in her mind that she was going to make it happen.

"Dakrhaeth," she called. The steadiness of her own voice surprised her. She recalled how Captain Milos had disabled the GSO's Cutlass. "I do not want any loss of life. I want to immobilize them or take out their weapons. So, let's go get them, one Drednot at a time."

"Thought you'd never ask, Mihaal," Dakrhaeth said.

Ramya glanced at Ross. He was scanning the buttons and levers spread out in front of him, and now he looked up at her. There was no anger in his eyes, only a steady resolve. Ramya was sure his anger hadn't vanished but that Ross had put it away for the moment.

"Let's do it," he said.

They were going to do it or die trying.

21

Two Drednots stood like sentinels near the AP, blocking the path to the SLH. Two others chased the *Endeavor*, blasting their way through the asteroid field as their quarry scuttled from the shelter of one rock to another. One definite advantage was the *Endeavor's* size and agility, and both came in particularly handy in the asteroid field. But the Drednots' weapons easily cleared a path through the maze of rocks.

Ramya drew a sharp breath when she saw a bright blast rip apart a chunky asteroid the size of a small moon to pieces. The *Endeavor* had thankfully moved away from behind its shelter or its shields would've taken a beating from the flying rock debris. One thing was clear: the *Endeavor's* clock was ticking down fast. A good hit could cripple the ship or even annihilate it.

They had to take out the Drednot leading the charge, Ramya thought, and then the next one following. She was sure that once the two Drednots were put out of action, the other two near the AP would join the hunt. Also, the moment the Drednots detected the Stryker, they'd come after it. But if the Stryker was quick enough or stealthy enough, they could create some room for the *Endeavor* to get back into the SLH.

She nudged the Stryker forward, hugging the rocks and keeping away from a direct line of sight from the Confederacy warships. They could easily pick up the Stryker's presence from a scan and they probably already had, but Ramya was not revealing herself unless she had to.

"Dakrhaeth, what weapons do you have on?" she asked the AI.

"Torpedoes," Dakrhaeth replied curtly.

There was a moment of stillness before Ross shot a disbelieving look at Ramya. She knew what he was thinking: *How could a fighter craft as advanced as this only have torpedoes?*

"And what else?" Ross finally asked.

There was a moment of silence, which Ramya found odd. AIs were supposed to be fast, weren't they?

"You'll find my Stinger torpedoes quite powerful, Ross," the AI replied. "However, discussing weapons is beside the point. I recommend paying more attention to the flying or slowing down."

Ramya hated to admit, but Dakrhaeth was correct. Asteroids — some pebble-sized, some almost as big as the Drednots — zoomed past the Stryker. If one were to hit the Stryker . . . Ramya quashed the fear. She was not alone. Dakrhaeth was with her.

The ease with which the Stryker maneuvered, almost caressing the curves of the rocks, yet never going close enough to get the proximity sensors blinking, Ramya was pretty sure Dakrhaeth was helping. *Good to have a backup,* she thought. As long as they got the job of saving the *Endeavor* done, she didn't care who helped her.

Ahead of them, the Drednot leading the attack fired a salvo off its ion cannon, and a brilliant flash later, two asteroids crumbled to pieces. For a second, the *Endeavor* was in the open, and then it ducked, scooting to find shelter behind the nearest rock. Ramya pushed the throttle to maximum and swung past the last asteroid that stood between the Stryker and a direct view of the leading Drednot's dorsal turrets.

"Mihaal," Dakrhaeth called. "We have a direct line of sight."

"I'm going to take out the ion cannons," Ramya declared.

"With torpedoes?" Ross asked, skepticism evident in his voice.

Dakrhaeth replied quickly, "Do not underestimate my torpedoes, please, Ross."

"That's 'Commander Ross' to you," Ross snapped.

"My mistake, Commander."

"All right, all right," Ramya cut in impatiently. Now was not the time for tending to bruised egos, not when the *Endeavor* was fighting for its life. She eased the Stryker forward, keeping a steady distance from the leading Drednot and its turrets. "Prep the torpedoes."

"Ready and prepped, Mihaal," came the instant reply.

Ramya breathed in deep. "All right, once we've taken these out, we have to get over to the other side and hit the other turrets."

"Not a good idea," Dakrhaeth quipped.

"What?" Ramya blurted, taking her thumb away from the red button of the torpedo launcher.

At that precise moment of indecision, bright white light flashed across the window. The Drednot had fired on the *Endeavor* again. The blast ripped an asteroid to shreds, and Ramya was sure a sizeable chunk of rock debris had hit the *Endeavor* seeing the way the ship shuddered. That did not look good. A shield would only hold up so long. There was no time to discuss strategy while the Drednot was bent on wiping out the *Endeavor*. That could wait until she had distracted the battleship a little.

Ramya placed her thumb back on the red button and gave it a firm press. A rumble spread under her feet and seconds later a blast enveloped the Drednot's turrets in a wave of light. *The shield has probably stopped it,* Ramya thought.

"Try another one, Mihaal," Dakrhaeth suggested.

Ramya pressed the launch button again, hoping the next torpedo would get through. It did. Another flash of light and the turret fell in pieces off the Drednot. Ramya heaved a sigh of relief. That'd buy them and the *Endeavor* a minute or two, at least.

"Explain, Dakrhaeth," she yelled, hugging the shadow of a large puckered rock. "Why isn't going for the other turrets a good plan?"

"Running around trying to destroy each of their weapons is not a realistic choice. There's not enough time and too many targets. Besides, we do not have an unending supply of torpedoes. Also, you've already attracted their attention," Dakrhaeth replied calmly. Sure enough, the second Drednot had turned their way. A blast of light fell on a large rock behind them and rock debris went flying past.

"Damn," Ramya cursed, diving to avoid the pieces.

"It's better if we target their engines or their reactor and disable them. They'd be as good as a space rock without those," Dakrhaeth said calmly.

That was a good plan except the Drednots had layers and layers of protection. Ramya had always enjoyed looking at the ship designs. Even after her father had stopped her from entering the Kiroff factories, she often hacked her way into the design department's archives and pored over the stacks of data. The Drednot was one of her favorite ships and she knew the reactor and the engine was pretty much unreachable. Trying to get to them would only be a waste of firepower. However, the engine . . .

"What the iffin hell, Rami?" Ross yelled.

Ramya blinked and stiffened. For a second, while she was trying to recall how the Drednot was built, she had drifted from the urgency of the situation. Thankfully, Ross had taken over the flying and the Stryker hopped and dodged and swerved to keep away from the blasts of energy that kept on coming.

Ramya shot a grateful look at her co-pilot. "Thanks," she muttered, and Ross responded with a curt nod.

"Next time, let me know before you switch off," he added.

"Don't worry, Ross," Dakrhaeth chimed in. "I'm always here. Monitoring the situation and . . . assisting."

It was obvious Dakrhaeth had been assisting. Like a shadow, he was bringing the weapons online, correcting flight paths, adjusting speed. Without him, they'd be lost. Ross however, didn't seem to appreciate the information.

"Any ideas?" he demanded.

"I was thinking . . . we can't directly hit the engine," Ramya replied breathlessly, "but we can take out the support pylons. That could severely impact the engines."

Ross shot a questioning glance. "How do you know this?"

Ramya hesitated. She couldn't simply tell him the Drednots were designed in factories owned by her father. Not at this moment.

She shrugged. "I'm just trying to guess here. It's standard battleship design."

"Hmm," Ross said. He pulled the flight stick and turned the Stryker to face the leading Drednot. As the craft turned, Ramya looked for the *Endeavor*, but she couldn't find it anywhere. "Since you obviously know more about the pylons, you want to take it from here?" Ross offered.

"All right." Ramya wrapped her fingers tightly around the flight stick. "Here goes."

Gritting her teeth, she pulled the direction controller backward as hard as she could to point the nose of the Stryker up, and then pressed on the throttle. The Stryker shot up. Once past the top of the Drednot, she swooped down, guns pointed at the pinched section at the back of the battleship where two sturdy arches — the support pylons — held up the core of the engineering section, including the reactors and the engines above them. If she could penetrate the shield and cause enough damage to one of the pylons, they'd cause enough trouble to the engines. Enough, at least, for the Drednot to give up chasing them.

She zoomed in close and just before pulling up the flight stick to straighten the Stryker, she pressed the torpedo launch button.

"Was that a hit?" she asked, busily turning the Stryker around.

"Yes, it was," Ross said, peeking outside and behind them. "These torpedoes are something else. They're tearing through the shields really easy."

Ramya had noted that also. When she had fired on the ion cannons, she hadn't expected them to fall apart so quickly. Battleships were built to withstand torpedoes; their shields could ward off fighter attacks for a long while. But not so much against the Stryker.

She circled the pylon, studying it intently for a moment. The last hit had partly deflected off the shield. She needed one more, a real good hit. Ramya took a quick look around before steadying the Stryker for the next attack. The two Drednots guarding the AP had not moved, but the second ship following them was drawing closer. Too damn close for comfort.

"Have to do this fast," she whispered, and fired the torpedo. The projectile streaked across space and slammed into the pylon, forming a fiery ball on one side. "Damn it!" Ramya howled. It wasn't as good a strike as she had hoped, and even though it had surprisingly torn through the shield, it didn't hit the girder at the center. And that meant she had to do it all over again.

Spinning the Stryker around to face the pylon, she steadied the craft and pressed the launcher button again. This time, the torpedo hit the pylon dead center and blasted a large hole through the metal.

"Yes!" Ramya shot a fist into the air. She could see the pylon twisting. It would crumble, and even if it didn't, the crew would have to focus more the collapsing engineering section rather than chasing the pair of rogue ships.

"That was unbelievably powerful. Either these Drednots are seriously underpowered or the AI was right about the torpedoes," Ross commented. "But I don't—"

"I'm *not* an AI, Commander Ross," Dakrhaeth corrected right away. "I'm—"

"Sorry," Ross cut Dakrhaeth off just as quickly. "Someone tell me where the hell is the *Endeavor*?"

Ramya's heart skipped a beat at Ross's question. In the heat of battle, she had forgotten all about the reason for the battle. Where was the *Endeavor*? The last she had seen it scuttling deeper into the asteroid field.

"Can you run a scan, Dakrhaeth?" Ross asked.

"Yes, Commander Ross."

"Let's head their way and take a look," Ramya said, pulling away from the crumbling pylon and heading into the asteroid field. She regretted leaving the shadow of the Drednot almost immediately. A rock blew up right behind her tail as soon as they had cleared the nose of the Confederacy battleship.

"Pull back, pull back right now!" Ross yelled. "The other ship is firing at us."

Ramya dived along the side of the first ship and under its belly. That had been a mistake. They would be safe only if they stayed close enough to a Confederacy ship, like now. But the thought of her own safety didn't make Ramya feel any better. Her heart sank as she fretted about the *Endeavor*. What was the point of hiding anyway if the *Endeavor* was already compromised? Without Captain Milos, how far could they go? This war was as good as lost.

"Anything?" Ross asked impatiently. "Any signs of the *Endeavor* yet?"

No one spoke.

Ramya suddenly realized her hands were as cold as ice. Without the *Endeavor*, they didn't stand a chance.

Ramya reeled. The darkness outside, the shadow of the behemoth hanging above them, the unending, lifeless space for as far as she could see, cast an endless shade over her mind.

She craved for some air . . . some light . . . warmth . . .

"I do. I see them," Dakrhaeth's voice drifted in. "It's the *Endeavor* . . . making its way to the AP in a rather circuitous way, possibly trying to avoid these battleships."

Ramya felt faint, but relief washed over her like a soft, warm wave.

"Are they all right?" Ross asked.

"They are still in one piece."

There could be a million other things wrong in the ship even if it were physically in one piece, but there was no point asking the AI. If the *Endeavor* was in one piece, it was good enough . . . for now.

"That's good," Ross said, letting out a long breath. "So, if they are heading toward the AP, then we have to keep these ships occupied so they'll have a chance to escape. But first we need to get out from under here."

He turned to look at Ramya. "You all right?" he asked, raising a quizzical eyebrow.

"Yes," Ramya replied, gulping to steady her voice. The shadow over her senses still lingered, but it was definitely clearing. Knowing that the *Endeavor* was functioning had helped. "What do we do now?"

"The ship above us seems as good as a dead, so we needn't worry about it," Ross said. "We need to get the second ship out of the way and then distract those two"—he pointed at the two Drednots that were still blocking the AP—"so the *Endeavor* can pass into the SLH."

"We can get the pylon of the next ship as well," Ramya suggested.

"Works for me," Ross replied. "Let's go."

Ramya kept under the belly of the disabled Drednot for as long as she could and then she shot out. The second Drednot must've been tracking the Stryker because a torpedo came streaking toward them no sooner than they were out of the first Drednot's shadow.

"Iffin hell," Ramya shouted, ducking behind a smallish rock to evade the projectile. In the next instant the asteroid broke into pieces, debris hurtling everywhere and over them.

"My shields are less than optimal," Dakrhaeth declared. "I suggest you take better evasive actions."

"I'm trying, I'm trying," Ramya said, tugging at the flight stick and weaving through the debris that streaked past them in a non-stop stream. She pressed the throttle as hard as she could, hoping to quickly take the Stryker past the dorsal guns to the vulnerable pylons in the midsection.

"The *Endeavor* is making good progress," Dakrhaeth announced. That was good news, but not that good. Even if these two Drednots were engaged, the two at the AP were not. The *Endeavor* would be able to go only so far unless she found a way to finish this Drednot and distract the ones guarding the AP.

"Can you try contacting the *Endeavor*?" Ross asked the AI.

"I have been trying," Dakrhaeth replied snippily. "Their tech continues to be . . . antiquated."

"Damn, look at those," Ross yelled suddenly. "Rami, watch out!"

The Stryker had been streaking past the Drednot, up along its length toward the pylons. As they passed, turrets were pushing out into place all along the side of the Drednot. There had to be about twenty gun mounts in all, a custom designed feature, Ramya was sure. The standard model Drednot did not come with such flank guns. Whether these were particle weapons or projectile weapons, she couldn't tell just by looking at them, but if as much as half of these turned in the direction of the Stryker and discharged, they'd do enough damage to the fighter. Perhaps destroy it altogether.

The only way to get out of the gun array's way was to dive down. Ramya pushed the flight stick forward and picked up speed as she sped forward, plunging below the Drednot's belly.

"Good move," Ross said. "Watch out," he shouted a moment later. The Drednot was starting to roll above them. This Drednot — quite unbelievably so — seemed to be much more agile than the first.

"Damn," Ramya muttered as the rail guns came into view once more. She pressed frantically at the throttle so she could get the Stryker as quickly as possible out of the guns' sight.

The Stryker hardly moved.

"Dakrhaeth," Ramya shouted. "What the hell is going on? Why can't we move?"

"They have their tractor beams locked on us."

"Can't we break free?" Ramya asked, jabbing at the throttle control.

"I'm afraid the beams are too strong."

The turrets were turning, all taking aim.

"The guns," Ross shouted. "Kill those guns before they shoot."

"How the hell do I kill all those guns?" Ramya shouted back.

"I don't know," Ross said. "I thought you knew standard battleship design."

These were not standard design. However, there was nothing novel about these gun arrays. About five guns were mounted in sets, and about twenty sets were distributed all along the flank of the Drednot.

Yes, she could kill one of the sets even while they were trapped in the tractor beam, but then the next set would fire at them. How many could she possibly hit anyway? *Stop overthinking*, Ramya chided herself, and pushed the torpedo launch button. The Stryker rumbled a bit and then an explosion ripped the nearest flank guns off the Drednot.

Ross breathed in relief. "Good, now torpedo the next one."

"That won't be possible," Dakrhaeth informed. "That was our last torpedo."

"What?" Ross shouted.

The next set of guns had started to swivel toward them.

"I don't carry an endless supply of torpedoes. That would not be mechanically possible to—"

"Dakrhaeth, stop!" Ramya interrupted. The Drednot's guns were almost in place. "What else can we use?" she asked.

"We have one weapon that could help, but . . ."

"But what?" Ramya shouted. "Whatever it is, deploy it now."

"It's a powerful plasma weapon, Mihaal," Dakrhaeth said. "May I remind you that you did not want loss of life, and using it would possibly cause loss of life."

Really? In another second or two at most, they'd be blasted into oblivion, and here she was, being lectured by an AI?

Before she could shout her order again, the Drednot's rail guns contracted slightly and fired. Projectiles hit the Stryker in an unending barrage. The Stryker swayed wildly, and if not for the tractor beams holding it, it would have been flung across the asteroid field. A warning light on the console flashed.

"Shields are suboptimal," Dakrhaeth informed.

All because *you* keep on yapping. Had the rail guns been particle weapons, they'd be fried and dead by now.

"Dakrhaeth!" Ramya yelled. "Bring up the plasma weapon. Now!"

There was an unnerving silence.

"Dakrhaeth!"

"Mihaal, I advise not using the plasma. It's quite . . . potent. It's also the last effective weapon we have. And it'll drain power quickly—"

"There's no other way, is there?" Ramya said through gritted teeth. "I said, bring them up."

A second of silence and then Dakrhaeth spoke, "Plasma vents online."

A section on the far left side of the console lit up, and Ramya recognized the layout. It was a weapon-control system specific to the plasma guns, which had obviously been kept offline until needed.

The shield warning flashed again, brighter this time.

"Shields at twenty-five percent," Dakrhaeth said.

They were losing . . . fast.

"Dakrhaeth, help me aim the plasma," Ramya said.

Another moment of silence fell. Then both Ross and Ramya yelled in unison. "Dakrhaeth!"

"Just noting, Mihaal, that might cause catastrophic damage," Dakrhaeth warned.

"The plasma will drain our power. How will we get away from them after we discharge?" Ross asked.

Ramya didn't know. First, they had to live through this, and the gunfire bombarding them nonstop didn't leave them much time. She knew it'd be a catastrophe that'd possibly claim lives of innocent people aboard the Drednots, something she wanted to avoid altogether. But *they* were trying to kill her, and that wasn't an option either. She was not done living her life yet.

"Aim it!" she ordered.

"Plasma vents aimed and ready," Dakrhaeth informed.

There was a chance that she'd breach the Drednot's hull altogether, depending on how much power the Stryker's plasma gun packed, and then there'd be the loss of life she wanted to avoid. But she didn't have a choice. They didn't leave her a choice. Gritting her teeth, Ramya fired.

She felt the Stryker shudder. Did it also feel a little warmer? Waves of energy flew out of the Stryker and rammed the Drednot's body. Before she could blink, the metal shattered and peeled. Debris flew through space as the behemoth tottered and sank below her.

Lifting her thumb off the gun controls, Ramya pulled the flight stick up, straightening the Stryker. The Stryker moved! They were free of the tractor beam!

This was her chance. Ramya wanted to look at the destroyed Drednot, but before that she had to get the Stryker away from there. She pressed on the throttle and the Stryker moved forward, but barely. Gone was the breakneck speed she'd gotten used to, the Stryker's movement was now more like the scramjets they used for training at the CAWStrat. And it was slowing even more.

Damn!

"Where's the *Endeavor*?" Ross asked.

"Approaching the AP," Dakrhaeth replied. "That's good timing since the Drednots guarding the AP are clearly interested in us now."

Ramya looked up. Dakrhaeth was right; the two Drednots that had stood guard next to the AP all along now moved forward. They were heading straight toward the Stryker. Her eyes lingered for a second over the shimmering outline of the AP beyond the two Drednots. They had to get there.

She pushed the throttle again. The Stryker barely moved. "Dakrhaeth?" she yelled. "Why aren't we moving yet?"

"The plasma discharge has drawn too much power," Ross said. "Have to wait longer before we get enough power to move again."

"The commander is correct."

In other words, they were truly, literally, a sitting duck.

Ramya blinked hard. The two Drednots guarding the AP were approaching head on, the red-striped flagship of Admiral Kanaa leading the way. How could she get past two of these attacking in unison? When she'd taken on the last two, she had the element of surprise on her side. But now they knew and they were coming straight for her Stryker. To top it all off, the Stryker still couldn't move.

Dread rose in thick clots to her throat and all Ramya wanted to do was scream. The Drednots lumbered forward, a hundred times bigger than the Stryker, their build reminding Ramya of a massive death machine that would crush her in a blink.

"Dakrhaeth," she yelled. "Do we have power yet?"

"About fifty percent, Mihaal," Dakrhaeth replied. "And by the way, the *Endeavor* just passed the AP."

Good! The *Endeavor* was finally safe, and fifty percent power was good enough. Ramya turned around, pushed the thruster to the maximum, and flew deeper the asteroid field in search of shelter. Flashes of light crisscrossed the space around her from time to time, sometime missing the Stryker narrowly, sometime distantly. It was only a matter of time, Ramya knew. Up and down, left and right — Ramya kept on darting. The onslaught didn't stop, and all Ramya did was evade. She was going farther and farther away from the AP and from a chance to escape.

A large button on the console blinked suddenly.

"They're hailing us," Ross whispered.

Ramya thought for a second. Then she slapped the button.

"Surrender," Admiral Kanaa's voice roared across the cockpit instantly.

"Never," Ramya hissed. Angry at herself that she'd accepted their call, Ramya was about to shut it off, the admiral chimed in again.

"You're surrounded," she said. "You can't escape."

Ramya turned around to look. There they were, two behemoths bearing down on them like a pair of primeval beasts.

"Never," Ramya shouted, bringing her fist down on the communication button. "Dakrhaeth, what weapons do we have left?"

A moment of hopeless silence seemed to stretch forever.

"Anything at all?" she asked again.

"Only rail guns, Mihaal."

"Bring them up," Ramya ordered.

"And do what? Those are—" Ross started to protest, but it was cut short when Ramya yanked the Stryker's flight stick and made the craft spin around and face the approaching Drednots.

"What are you doing, Rami?" Ross yelled.

She was planning to give them a fight they'd remember.

"I'm going to try something, Ross. Won't be pretty. Sure as hell, won't be safe," Ramya blurted. "You with me?"

Ross inhaled sharply. "Go for it," he said.

"All right then," Ramya said, running her tongue over her rapidly drying lips. "We'll cut a path right through the middle of the two."

Ramya heard the Stryker's rumble as she pressed on the throttle. She pulled the craft up and they shot toward the Drednots. Blasts shot out in the darkness they'd just left behind. Ramya's heart pounded faster and faster. She pushed the throttle to the max; the Stryker streaking forward in a path that lay between the two Confederacy ships.

"Help me, Dakrhaeth," Ramya screamed. "Get us between the two. Faster."

"We *are* at maximum speed, Mihaal," Dakrhaeth replied coolly. "I'll keep it at that. But I must caution that you're getting closer to them and that is as good as making a death wish."

"It's our only chance," Ramya said. The only safe zone lay between the two ships. As long as the Stryker was in the middle, they couldn't shoot at it, since that would mean shooting at each other. Ramya only hoped they wouldn't catch on her plan too quickly.

The two Drednots were following the Stryker's trajectory, blasts of energy lighting up a trail behind them. Ramya didn't believe they could fall for it, but both ships were slowly starting to turn toward each other. A bit more and then . . . if they wanted to keep firing at the Stryker, they'd have to face each other. And when they realized they were in each other's line of fire, they'd have to stop. That would be her chance to shoot past them and get into the SLH. She only had a few seconds to make this happen.

"Help me, Ross," Ramya yelled. "Keep a straight course to the AP."

What if the warships turned quicker and one Drednot got out of the other's way? What if they turned some special missile loose on them? Nothing was impossible in a battle.

"Faster. Go faster," she whispered, pushing the throttle flat against the dashboard. She hastily wiped away the sweat that had trickled down her forehead and into her eyes.

The shimmery outline of the AP looked like a possibility, if only she could make it past the tail end of the Drednots.

"They're turning around now," Ross said with a quick look backward.

"We can make it," Ramya said through gritted teeth. It was starting to look better. And possible. Ramya turned around to check on the Drednots behind them. The one to their left had almost straightened itself.

"Faster, damn it," she shouted, pushing down her numb finger on the throttle with her other hand.

"Good news, Mihaal," Dakrhaeth spoke suddenly.

They could all use some good news now. "What is it?" Ramya blurted.

"Ancillary power has reached optimal level. We can now use a turbo boost on our thrusters."

"What the hell are you waiting for?" Ross growled.

"Mihaal?"

"Yes, Dakrhaeth! Anything to make us go faster," Ramya shouted. From the corner of her eye, she saw a bolt of energy streaking toward them.

They had made it. Almost. If they could dodge that fire.

"Ross?" Ramya squawked.

"Got it," Ross replied, and the Stryker plunged downward. The beam of fiery light passed over them.

Ramya felt a light rumble around her and the Stryker jolted forward. The turbo mode was engaged. It was now or never. She pushed the throttle flat on the dashboard.

The AP loomed ahead.

"Dakrhaeth, switch to Super Luminal mode," Ramya yelled. "Dakrhaeth, you copy?"

"Yes, Mihaal, it's done."

Another vivid flash streaked past the Stryker. Ramya gritted her teeth and pushed on the throttle. The Stryker careened through the AP into the SLH.

They were safe!

Ramya fell back into her seat, eyes closed, cradling her sore finger. For a while she simply breathed, noisily. They had made it.

"Mihaal, I set a temporary destination to Kamma so we can shake the Confederacy ships off our tail. But where do you really want to go?" Dakrhaeth interrupted her momentary peace almost immediately.

Right! They had to go somewhere. She had won against those colossal battleships, but this she had no clue about. She didn't even know the nearby star systems, let alone where they could go.

Ross has to know. Ramya shot a questioning look at her co-pilot who sat heaving in his seat, staring blankly ahead.

"Ross," Ramya started tentatively. "Where do we go from here?"

He didn't look at her, instead scanned the instruments in front of him.

"Ross?"

"I'm trying to think," he said. "We can't be flying around on our own. Not in this ship. We have to find the *Endeavor.*"

Didn't she know that? The Stryker, with its unusual looks, would draw attention instantly. And even if they had somehow managed to outsmart the Confederacy this time, she knew the next time they wouldn't be as lucky. The next time the Confederacy would send twenty ships, if not more. The next time, they might not have an asteroid field to take cover. Besides, her father and his GSO minions would be on the lookout as well. No good could come from flying around in the Stryker.

But where would they find the *Endeavor*? At last glance, the old ship had seemed battered to her. The hull had taken a beating. Would it even survive a flight through the SLH?

"Dakrhaeth," Ross called, "show us the star systems nearest to Totori. And ones with . . . habitable planets."

"Of course."

The display unit that was set over the control panel lit up with a map showing star clusters, two spots blinking yellow.

"The blinking spots are stars with habitable planets, Commander Ross. The Tessereth is closest to Totori, with two planets in the habitable zone: Alun-Fae and Gorro. The other one, the Kashiyap, has only one planet that's habitable. The Morris II. That—"

"Morris II? Isn't that a Mwandan sanctuary?"

"It is said to have a native Mwandan population, yes," replied Dakrhaeth.

Ramya listened intently. She knew of Morris II well. Morris Jakumbe was the first human to come into contact with the Mwandans, a sentient species that flourished in the galaxy from before the humans had settled. The Mwandans were considered part of the Confederacy, even though they were reclusive to a fault and never participated in Confederacy matters.

"That's where we'll go," Ross declared. "Take us to Morris II, Dakrhaeth."

Ramya sat up and looked at Ross. "What? I thought Mwandans disliked humans. I thought the Confederacy had a rule against entering Mwandan habitats."

"Yes, they do," Ross replied. "That's why I think the captain will go there."

"You think?"

Ross sighed. Then he turned slowly to look her in the eye. "I *know*. It's the perfect place to hide. It's also the perfect place to repair the ship without intrusions."

Or the perfect place to die. Mwandans could be unfriendly if they chose to, deadly even. Taking the Stryker there was . . .

"Mihaal?" Dakrhaeth asked. Clearly, he wasn't taking an order from Ross without making sure Ramya approved it.

Ramya shot another glance at Ross. He seemed confident, although guessing from his tight jaw, a tad irritated at the questioning. Ross knew Captain Milos much more than she did. If he was sure the captain would take the *Endeavor* to Morris II, Ramya had to trust his judgment. But it was also likely they'd be attacked by the Mwandans. Either way, she had to choose. And death was a possibility no matter what she chose.

"Take us to Morris II, Dakrhaeth," Ramya said.

"As you wish, Mihaal," the AI replied. "One hour thirty-six minutes to Morris II."

One hour thirty-six minutes!

Ramya fell back in her seat and closed her eyes. One hour thirty-six minutes. That was all she could be sure about. What would happen after that was anybody's guess.

An Excerpt

The First Covenant

(Dark Universe Series - Book 2)

Ground cover had a different meaning on Morris II, Ramya realized as soon as the Stryker approached the surface of the planet. The vegetation—wide swaths of plants in all sorts of shapes and sizes— had dark foliage and there was barely a spot or two of the ground not covered by it. The dim light of the star made the entire scenery murky and depressing.

Dakrhaeth steered the Stryker steadily in the direction of the explosion they had seen earlier and Ramya could barely think straight. She didn't hope for much. Better to prepare for the worst— the Endeavor had crashed and no one had survived. But even considering that didn't clear her head. She still couldn't think beyond finding the crash site and it didn't help that Ross sat rigid and stony-faced next to her, refusing to speak.

She wasn't going to give in to him, Ramya thought irritably. He could fret and fume as much as he wanted. Her eyes were glued on the landscape below, the thudding of her heart growing steadily like a war-drum beating faster and louder as the time of first encounter drew near. As time crawled past they crossed more ground, but there was no sign of a crashed spacecraft.

"I'm locked on the explosion site, Mihaal."

Ramya sucked in some air and braced for the inevitable. The Endeavor would be in pieces and everyone in it—dead.

She reached for the flight stick. No one could alter the grim truth, but at least being in charge when facing it would give some sense of control even when there was none.

"I'll take over Dakrhaeth," she announced. Grabbing the flight stick, she leaned forward to look outside. A thick plume of smoke rose a short distance away, right from the middle of the dark expanse of the forest. Dakrhaeth had scopes and sensors at his disposal to see more, Ramya figured.

"What do you see, Dakrhaeth?" she asked, ignoring the throbbing lump that seemed to keep expanding in her throat.

"It is interesting. I do not see any spacecrafts. A building seems to be on fire."

The breath Ramya had been holding made out of her in a slow relaxed wave. There was still hope! Maybe the Endeavor had landed somewhere safely. Maybe its crew was still alive. Regardless, they needed to check out the explosion site and make sure it had nothing to do with the Endeavor.

Ramya pointed the Stryker's nose directly to the swirling gray column. As the Stryker drew closer to the plume, she saw the source of the smoke clearly. Dakrhaeth was correct—there was no spacecraft in sight. At the center of the site was a building complex of some sort, built of a dark-brown material. The centermost structure was shaped like an ovoid. An explosion had ripped it in half and smoke billowed out of it. Ramya could see the raging fire and people—Mwandans were humanoids, so they looked just like regular people from afar— ran in and out of the area.

"Mihaal, they're looking. I suggest we get out of here." Dakrhaeth sounded a cautionary note.

"I agree," Ramya muttered under her breath as she tugged the flight stick to turn the Stryker around. There was no Endeavor here, so whatever else was going on down there was none of her business.

"Watch out!" Ross shouted.

Ramya tugged on the flight stick and pressed hard on the throttle, but it was already too late. Something hit the right side of the Stryker in a series of soft plops. It didn't sound harmful yet the craft tipped sideways and the alarms went blaring.

Ramya threw her weight on the flight stick and pushed the

throttle down. The Stryker turned and pulled forward but not as quickly as Ramya wanted it to. Her vision was blurred and world seemed to recede from her, but Ramya held on. By the time they'd cleared the vicinity of the explosion site Ramya was gasping for air. It had to be the rush of adrenaline, or maybe it was her empty stomach. For the most part though, it was the alarms that seemed to assault her senses with their unending screech. The entire control panel was blinking red, as if everything on the Stryker was falling apart.

"Dakrhaeth," Ramya shouted as soon as she had made some distance between them and the building. "What happened? How bad are we hit?"

The alarms quietened abruptly. The silence that followed told Ramya there could be nothing good to hear.

-End of excerpt-

About the Author

Alex Sheppard has always wanted to be an author. And even though that dream eluded Alex for a long time, now, finally, the ducks seem to have lined up. This is the first of Alex's space opera series.

When not obsessively guzzling books (mostly scifi), tinkering with gadgets and gizmos, and wrangling rambunctious little ones, Alex likes to write.

Want to follow Alex's adventures in the writing world? Check out https://thefarworlds.com.